THREE DREAMS
and a NIGHTMARE

and Other Tales of the Dark

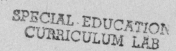

THREE DREAMS
and a NIGHTMARE
and Other Tales of the Dark

JUDITH GOROG

Troll Associates

◆ *For* ◆

Grandmother and Grandfather Kelley,
whose adventures deserve an entire shelf of books.

A TROLL BOOK, published by Troll Associates,
Mahwah, NJ 07430

Published by arrangement with The Putnam & Grosset Group.
For information address The Putnam & Grosset Group,
51 Madison Avenue, New York, New York 10010.

First Troll Printing, 1989

Printed in the United States of America.

10 9 8 7 6 5 4 3 2 1

ISBN 0-8167-1822-9

CONTENTS

Jacob's Dream: An Introduction
9

Mall Rat
13

First dream: The Ugly Mug
21

The Perfect Solution
35

The Mirror
41

Three Grains of Rice:
from the Bones of an Arab Folktale
51

Prosperity
57

Second Dream: Carlo the Silent
65

Hedwig the Wise
73

Sad Eyes
81

At the Sign of the Beckoning Finger
95

Third Dream: The Price of Magic
101

In Her Belfry
121

Overture
129

And a Nightmare
151

Inside My Head

In my head,
there's a perfect world,
inside my head.
Inside my head,
I can sing
and kick that goal
inside my head.
And the swing goes high,
and never runs
down
Inside my head.

Jacob's Dream:
An Introduction

*T*here is a story told in a book sacred to three of the religions on the planet earth. It is an old story, a story about a worried man and the dream he had.

A certain man, whose name was Jacob, was journeying to meet, after many years, with his brother. Jacob had reason to fear their meeting, for he had wronged his brother before they had parted. And Jacob thought as he walked, for in that time and place people generally traveled on foot, and Jacob thought of how he could diminish his brother's anger. Jacob traveled slowly toward the meeting, sending ahead gifts to his brother. He sent ahead flocks of sheep and goats, and servants, placing as many people and animals as possible between himself and his brother, putting off the moment of their meeting.

Jacob put himself behind his wives and children as he delayed the meeting. Night fell. Jacob lay down to sleep, and it seems he simply lay down upon the earth, with only his cloak for a cover, with all the stars of the desert sky above him, and a rock for a pillow beneath his head. And as Jacob slept, he dreamed that a being came to him and that they wrestled, wrestled all night long, and Jacob dreamed he wrestled so long and so well that even as the dawn came, they were still struggling. And as the dawn came it was clearly seen that the being was an angel, who asked to be released, saying that he must depart before daylight. Jacob replied, in the poetic language of the translation that has come down to us, "I will not let thee go except thou bless me!"

And so the angel did.

Jacob stood up that morning with a pain in his hip, from which he limped all the rest of his life, for at one point in that long wrestling match with an angel Jacob had been thrown quite hard upon the ground.

Jacob awoke that morning and prayed and prepared to walk forward to meet his brother.

We are not told what Jacob expected his blessing to bring. One thing is certain—the blessing Jacob received did not protect him from suffering and sorrow. No, that does not seem to be the way of blessings.

MALL RAT

Have you heard about Rita who broke the rule? Normally, Rita was a regular girl. She brushed her teeth after every meal, always fastened her seatbelt, handed in her homework on time, and they loved her in the giftshop at the Mall. That's where Rita had an after-school job, in the giftshop at the Mall.

But.

But Rita hated locking the car doors. Rita hated all locked doors. They made her feel scared, left out. And what if she accidentally locked the keys in the car? So, even though her mother always told her, even though her father always told her, whenever she borrowed her mother's car or her father's car to drive to work at the Mall, Rita never locked the car doors.

Rita's trouble began one bitterly cold night just before Christmas. She'd worked clear up till closing time, and then a bit past, helping Melanie, the store manager, to tidy up and then close the giftshop. By the time they walked down to the employees' entrance, the big iron gates were already shut, the huge Mall dark.

Stan, the security man, sat by the door, chewing on a matchstick, saying goodnight to the last of the stragglers. Soon he'd lock the door and settle down with a fresh matchstick to watch the television screens on which flickered the dim corridors of Stan's section of the Mall.

"If you'll wait, ladies," Stan drawled, "Herbie'll be back and walk you to your cars."

"No. No thanks, Stan," Melanie replied. "My car's right there, right under that light. That's my own spot; get it every day."

Rita, whose car was quite far away said not a word, but shrugged, not wanting to seem helpless. After all the parking lot was full of bright lights.

Rita, who had begun to think of how her car doors were not locked, and of how far away her car was parked, silently followed Melanie out of the employees' entrance. Melanie chattered brightly while they walked to Melanie's car. Rita paused there a moment, while Melanie unlocked the door of her car. "Night, Rita," Melanie said. "See you tomorrow, and thanks again for the extra help. You're a doll!"

Rita smiled at the praise, then waved as Melanie drove away. It was a long way to the car, and the parking lot was so vast, so empty. Her shoes made hardly any sound in all that space. Rita shrank into her coat. Not a soul in sight. Above her a giant light hummed.

There, just a few steps more and she'd be in the car. Oh, it would be so cold inside the car and it would take ages to get warm.

What if it didn't start?

Stop it. Rita nearly said the words aloud.

Then, chuckling to herself, she did speak.

"You'll scare yourself to death," she admonished herself in just the tone her mom would use. But the sound of her own words in her mom's own tone sounded spooky in that empty space. Rita shuddered and walked faster.

There. There was the car, the door handle cold in her hand. Rita lifted the handle, prepared to dive inside. Then she'd lock the doors, start the engine, turn on the radio to drive away the scared feelings, get warm, and next time she'd come earlier to work so she could drive around to find a parking place closer to the entrance. And she'd definitely lock the car doors, too, not let herself be scared.

Rita was halfway into the car when she knew it. A smell? What? Cigarettes? Something. And a shape! Someone was inside the car. Rita jumped backwards, half falling out of the car, holding onto the car door.

"Sorry, dear," a dry little voice said from the passenger seat beside the driver. "It was so cold, and I missed my bus. Could you please give an old lady a ride home?"

Rita bent down to look inside the car. White hair stuck out from beneath a knitted cap adorned with a large gold pin, a rooster with bits of colored glass glittering in the plumes of his tail. The lights of the parking lot showed it all, an old lady in the front seat of Rita's mother's car, an old lady in a heavy wool coat and knitted gloves that didn't match her hat, an old lady with an enormous handbag on her knees.

Rita wanted to laugh. But still, she'd been so startled. Her heart still pounded at double its usual rate. Still.

"A ride home?" said Rita slowly. "Sure, but let me run back to give in the register key. I accidentally took it, and they'll need it to open tomorrow."

Before the old woman could reply, Rita closed the car door and ran back to the employees' entrance. It was locked.

Rita pushed the red button to ring the bell inside.

"Please, please, Stan. Open the door. Don't have gone to the toilet or for food. Please, please, be here."

It was so cold. Rita glanced back at the car. Was the car door opening?

She couldn't take anyone home, even an old lady. That

was a promise she couldn't break. It was late, so late. If only the door to the store would open, she'd call home.

Again and again she pressed the red button.

Finally. Stan opened the door; Rita pushed inside. It was warm, a bit stuffy even. Rita trembled as she told Stan about the old woman.

"Probably harmless," he drawled. "We're always getting them. Come here. Run out of money . . . or forget what time the last bus goes. Police will give her a ride home. They're due here any second now on their drive-through." Stan talked with somebody on his radio-phone while Rita used the pay-phone to call home. By the time she had hung up the receiver, Stan was grinning at her. "See. Here they are." She had stopped trembling; probably it had been from the cold. Imagine, scared by a little old lady!

"Hey, Herbie! You stay here. I'll walk Rita out to her car." Stan heaved his great bulk once more out of his chair and waddled out with Rita, out toward her mother's car. A policeman opened the door on the passenger side and offered his hand to the old lady.

"Sure M'am. We'll take you home. No problem. This little girl can't do it. She's late already and will be in trouble with her folks."

"Wellll, all right," the old woman whined. Slowly she turned in the seat, put both feet out of the car and leaned heavily on the policeman's arm as she limped slowly over to the police car.

Rita felt mean. After all, she could have telephoned to say she had to help an old lady. Just plain mean, that's all she was.

Stan stood beside the car while Rita started the engine. "You did the right thing," he said. "Even old ladies can be a bit peculiar. What if she decided she'd rather live with you than go home, huh? I've heard of it. Go safe now."

Rita, suddenly feeling more tired than ever before, drove out of the parking lot, toward the access road, swearing to herself that never, never, ever would she leave the doors unlocked again.

Just before the access road Rita glanced at the passenger seat. A lumpy newspaper lay where the old woman had been sitting. Rita could still see the prints and folds in the newspaper made by the old woman's bottom and by the shapes of what lay on the car seat. Slowing down for the red light at the highway, Rita lifted a corner of the newspaper.

It wasn't possible.

Rita tried to be calm, but killed the engine while stopping the car. Breathing very slowly, Rita took the newspaper entirely off the car seat. There, where they had been covered by the newspaper, where the old woman had sat on them. . . . There were the blades glittering in the light that fell from the corner lamp. Rita stared, and forced herself to breathe still more slowly. "An axe, a saw, a hammer, and a knife." Rita paused, ". . . an old lady with a gaudy rooster pin."

Rita turned to look back at the Mall. There was no one in sight. Opening her own car door, she got out, walked around the car, and opened the passenger door. Using the newspaper so that she would not need to touch them, Rita bundled up and lifted the axe, the saw, the hammer, and the knife off of the car seat and onto the grass beside the road.

Then Rita closed the car door, walked back around the car and got in on the driver's side. She started the engine and drove home, and as she drove she reasoned in the following way: "If I tell anyone about those things, then I'll be even later getting home tonight. I have already told my parents that I am late because of work. I did not mention the old woman or the unlocked car doors. If I tell, my parents will make me quit my job at the Mall, even if I swear to lock my doors. I will lock them, so I won't tell."

Rita did not tell.

Rita went home, and she didn't tell. Rita went back to work, and she locked her car doors.

Christmas passed, and at the giftshop they said she was such a good worker and such a help and wouldn't she like to work Saturdays and Thursday nights till summer when they'd have her work full-time.

And Rita worked, and whenever she borrowed her mother's car or her father's car, she always locked the doors. Locking the car doors as she did, Rita felt safe.

It was a warm night during the February thaw, when Rita left the Mall needing neither hat, nor scarf, nor gloves to keep her warm. Rita was completely comfortable in only a light jacket, with the carefree feeling such warm weather brings. She sang while she walked to her car.

Rita unlocked the door and got inside. Rita locked the car door, started the engine. But it was so warm; Rita opened the window for the fine, fresh air. Soon it would be spring.

Rita bent forward to turn on the car radio, heard that dry little voice at the open window.

"Hello, dearie. I've come for my things."

First Dream

THE UGLY MUG

The mug first existed in the dream of a boy, an apprentice potter, van Horn by name. He was as lively and cheerful a chap as ever you would hope to meet, but he used to dream of riches and glory.

In one of those dreams, van Horn took up a lump of clay and placed it on the potter's wheel. There, as the wheel gently spun, the clay formed a slender goblet from which silver and gold poured forth at van Horn's feet. At that, van Horn seized his dream and held tight. The goblet cried out, as if in pain, but van Horn did not let go. "I'll release you," he promised, "if you bless me!"

"Yes," replied the dream. "Yes. I'll bless you. From this day forward you shall become van Horn the Master Potter. Princes and emperors will pay great sums to you for your creations."

"Ah," sighed van Horn. "That is a blessing worth having," and he released the dream.

"Remember, van Horn!" warned the dream, its shape shifting and changing before his eyes until the goblet had become an ungainly, mournful portrait mug. "Remember," repeated the mug, "generosity cannot wear out the blessing."

"I'll remember," promised van Horn.

The blessing proved true. From that day van Horn had a touch more deft, a hand more sure, an eye for purity of line such as no other potter had. Under van Horn's hands, the clay became silky smooth, with never an air bubble to spoil it. His finished pieces were wonderfully thin, remarkably fine. Translucent bowls became his trademark. No one else could create such bowls, each one glazed in a rare and different shade of white, from the grey tints of storm clouds to the white-pink of a fine pearl. Each of his works was desired; each one was treasured, and van Horn became rich and famous.

That young and fortunate potter married well, and had a healthy little son, but as his wealth increased, van Horn more and more neglected the condition of his blessing, his duty as a human to be generous.

"No time for that nonsense!" van Horn was often heard to say. He had no time to listen to a friend, no time to lend a hand. Van Horn was known for his craftsmanship, for his temper, and for the fists he closed around his gold.

The blessing ended suddenly, in one brief day. From the minute van Horn entered the pottery that morning, the clay resisted him. Red-faced, van Horn cursed the trembling apprentice for his incompetence. "You!" he bellowed. "Get out! This clay is unfit to use. I'll prepare it myself! Go!" But when van Horn struggled to impose his will upon the unyielding grey mass, the clay eluded his fingers. It twisted, formed itself as van Horn watched in anger that became fear. The clay writhed into a dreadful shape that burst into flame, glowed hot. Colors blazed forth, garish colors van Horn had never used. The object cooled, all in minutes.

What stood on his worktable was a mug of surpassing ugliness. Large and lopsided, the whole of it was a mournful portrait face, the features distorted by sorrow. Its eyes drooped; deep furrows marked its cheeks. Two great ears were its handles. Van Horn stared at it in revulsion.

The ugly mug opened its huge mouth and began to shout, "Down! Down! Everything down!" Upon this order, the shelves lining the walls of the pottery collapsed. Down crashed the work of weeks. The great kiln, cooling after the three-day fire that produced van Horn's famous glazes, split its sides and crumbled to the ground. Tumbling bricks crushed the fragile pieces that rested inside.

When all was destroyed, only one single piece of pottery remained whole, the ugly mug. It had formed itself, had called down destruction, and now van Horn was determined to crush it. Taking it in his great hands, he hurled it against the wall. The mug remained whole, and spoke once again.

"Van Horn. Don't you recognize me? You neglected the condition of your blessing. It is taken from you."

With that, van Horn's hands, which had been both powerful and supple, twisted into tightly closed fists, each with a gold coin inside, a coin van Horn could not open his hands to release.

"Though I'm ruined," van Horn shouted, "I'll not have your face to mock me!" and he kicked the mug out the open pottery door.

Because van Horn was known for his temper, neither his wife nor his son had paid much attention to the shouting, not even to the sounds of destruction coming from the pottery. The man was known to shout, and to smash things in his anger.

Still, his little son was surprised to see the ugly mug come rolling out the pottery door and into the garden. The boy picked it up, and immediately made two decisions: He *must* have the mug for his own, but he would only ask his father's permission to keep it *after* dinner, when Master van Horn's mood was most likely to be mellow.

Young van Horn wiped the mug clean on his shirt and

carried it into the kitchen, which was empty. Carefully putting the mug into the cupboard, young van Horn went to look for his mother. Mistress van Horn came into the kitchen not long after, without having seen her son. She prepared a tray with fresh, clean grape leaves and piled it high with fruit. On such a beautiful day they would eat their midday meal outside under the trees, where the breeze would be cool.

She opened the cupboard and jumped back, startled, when she saw the mug. "Funny old thing," she said. "Who on earth could have made that? The apprentice?" As she took it down to look at it more carefully, there was a knock at the door. Mistress van Horn stepped out to see a weary beggar leaning on his crutch. The left sleeve of his jacket was sewn up to the shoulder, empty. Likewise his right trouser leg was sewn up above the knee, empty. In spite of his affliction, he had the appearance of strength, a certain weary cheerfulness. Perhaps it was the battered hat on his head, to which he had attached a sprig of borage. Around his shoulders he had slung a sort of sack. Something inside it moved.

"Good afternoon, Mistress," began the beggar. "I am an ex-soldier just returned from the recent war. I am strong and can easily chop that pile of branches into kindling for you in exchange for a meal."

"Of course," said Mistress van Horn. "We always need help. But wait. Isn't that a baby in your sling? May I see her? How do you come to have her?"

"She's my daughter," he replied, carefully taking the baby from the sack. "She's a bit wet," he added.

"No matter. We have dry cloths," said Mistress van Horn, taking the baby from him. "Of course, I can tell from her eyes she's a daughter. Haven't I longed to have one of my own?"

With that, Mistress van Horn set food and drink before the soldier. While he ate, she found a dry cloth and changed the baby, then fed her bread sops and soup from the ugly mug. The baby ate, smiled, and slept. The soldier, in response to the questions she asked, told Mistress van Horn his story, which began with his having been taken up to serve in the war and ended upon his return home, badly wounded, to find his wife dying, their infant daughter in her arms.

Upon finishing his meal, and the pipe Mistress van Horn insisted would aid his digestion, the soldier set to work on the wood. Mistress van Horn went to her trunks and cupboards to find a change of clothing for the baby. She then bathed the child when she awoke, and gave her milk from the ugly mug.

Finally the soldier made ready to depart. Three times he thanked Mistress van Horn and three times refused her offers of a home and work, saying, "I must go to my wife's family to tell them of her death, and then I must make a new home for my daughter and me. Thank you for your kindness, and bless you." With that, the soldier put his daughter once more into the sling.

"Here," said Mistress van Horn. "Take this mug for your daughter. Look at how she smiles at its silly, sad face. I pray it will always hold food and drink for her."

The soldier waved goodbye and limped away out of the courtyard and onto the road. Mistress van Horn returned to the kitchen, to the preparations for dinner for her family.

Young van Horn, who had been delayed by the distractions of orchard, barn and garden, returned to the kitchen a few minutes later.

"Mama!" he exclaimed when he came inside the kitchen. "Papa was shouting and things were crashing in the pottery and out came the most wonderful mug! It has a face going all around its front, with huge ears for handles, and hair glazed black and grey on the back of it . . . and such a sad face . . ." He reached into the cupboard. "But it's gone! Did Papa take it back?" The child began to cry. "Did he break it? I wanted to ask him for it."

"No. I saw it, and loved that sad face, and it delighted the baby." said Mistress van Horn. "I wondered how it got here, and never thought it was yours. I have just this minute given it away, to a poor soldier carrying his baby daughter." She pointed the direction in which they had gone.

"No! Not that one! Here, I'll give them this one." Reaching into the cupboard, young van Horn grabbed a silver cup. "I must get back that mug!" he shouted, running out the door. Though he went quite a long way on the road outside their house, young van Horn did not find the soldier. Much later, dusty and tired, his face streaked with tears, he returned home.

The boy dreamed that night of the ugly mug, dreamed the mug called to him.

For young van Horn, the days that followed were marked by hunger and the sorrow of seeing his father sit, crippled and silent, in the corner of the kitchen. In no time at all the riches amassed by the great Master Potter van Horn were gone, as if into the air. Mistress van Horn was quick to secure work sewing and mending, which gave them meager bread.

And the soldier, the baby, and the mug: How did their life go? When Mistress van Horn handed the mug to the ex-soldier, the baby reached out for it with both hands. There, inside the sling, she babbled to it while her father limped along the dusty road.

Their first piece of good fortune was that a farmer driving a wagon came along before they had gone thirty steps.

That farmer offered a ride to a spot a bit past the next village. Because there remained several hours of daylight, the soldier got down from the wagon, thanked the farmer, and continued his way on foot.

Just before nightfall he stopped to rest beneath a willow that stood between the road and a stream running alongside. There he and the baby had a supper of the food Mistress van Horn had packed for their journey. After their meal, they slept. The next morning, while they ate the last of the food given them by Mistress van Horn, a very old man came up the road, stopping beside them to rest. The ex-soldier, who had seen enough of hunger to recognize it without a word being said, handed the old man pieces of bread and cheese, inviting him to join them for breakfast. The old man accepted, chewed slowly "to make it last," thanked them, and continued on his way. After he had gone, the soldier prepared to put the baby once again into her carrying sling. The baby meanwhile had been exploring among the roots of the willow. With a cry of delight, she brought out something from the ground and put the edge of it into her mouth. With a baby's disregard for the moss and dirt clinging to it, she chewed away.

It took some time for the ex-soldier to convince the baby to exchange the gritty lump for the ugly mug. Finally the ex-soldier held it in his hands. Where the baby had chewed, he could already see the metal. It was a coin, gold, of great value. Perhaps a traveller had lost it. Perhaps a robber had buried it there.

Not many years later, young van Horn felt he was old enough to leave home. He went, not as an apprentice potter, not bound as any kind of apprentice, but simply walked out into the world to find work. When his mother asked why, and where would he go, young van Horn said, "I'll work, and send to you whatever money I can. Two things I hope to find along the way: Do you remember Mistress Ghalt saying her cousin had brought a wonderful salve? When she rubbed it into her crippled hands, they were free of pain and she could move them almost as well as before her sickness. I want to find such a salve to cure Papa. And . . ." he blushed.

"And?" repeated his mother.

"I dream of that old ugly mug. Do you remember the one Papa made the day . . ."

"That mug!" shouted the old man. "I never made it. It cursed me!"

"Papa," replied the boy. "I dream that mug holds all my happiness."

"Dreams!" snorted old van Horn, returning to his seat by the fireplace.

With that, young van Horn set out, crossing land and sea, spending freezing nights in dark forests, dry, windy days under the blazing sun, knowing both hunger and thirst. Along the way he found work, every kind of work, from cleaning stables and caring for animals to keeping books in a shipyard. His own needs were modest, so that, of what he earned, there was always enough to send a portion to his parents.

His journey to find the salve and the ugly mug was made particularly long and difficult because he began by making two mistakes: the first was to think that, because the salve he wanted for his father's hands was good, it must have come from the opposite side of the world. That mistake cost him years of travel, some hunger, and much discomfort. The second mistake was to think that an ex-soldier with one arm and one leg could only live alone and only by begging. Young van Horn gave a coin to each and every beggar he met. After every coin he asked the same question:

"Have you met a beggar with one arm and one leg who carries a mug that looks like this?" He then showed a drawing of the ugly mug as it appeared to him in his dreams. Every beggar took the coin with joy, glanced at the drawing, and then offered his own mug or bowl for sale instead.

Young van Horn never once found a single beggar who had seen the ex-soldier, nor the ugly mug, which only shows that you won't find something by looking in the wrong place.

During his years of travel and work, young van Horn looked and listened, read and thought. It was, therefore, no ordinary young man who rode late one afternoon into a small town in his very own country, a town just a two-day journey from his parents. The leaves shimmered crimson and golden in the last rays of autumn sunset. Young van Horn rode to a small shop on the edge of town, arriving somewhat past the normal closing time for shops in that village; a light nevertheless still shone inside the shop. Seeing that light, young van Horn sighed with relief. He could ask once more about the salve for his father's hands, once more before he looked for supper and a warm bed against the cold night to come. Dismounting, he tied his horse to a nearby post, and giving it an affectionate pat on the neck, left the animal looking about for something to nibble.

Three small bells on the door tinkled pleasantly when young van Horn entered the shop. He lost his heart before they were still. The girl writing labels at the end of the counter was able to look up and say, "Good evening. May I help you?" before her heart, too, had left its accustomed spot.

After stammering in and out of his sentences at least three times, young van Horn managed, "It's my father. His hands are wasted with disease. We have heard of a salve that takes away the pain and will let him use his hands again. Do you have such a thing?" While his words stumbled, his heart and mind raced: How can anyone have eyes of such extraordinary shades of brown, and auburn hair that holds the sun after it has set, and. . . ?

Putting down her work, the girl replied. "Yes. There is such an ointment. My father is preparing it now. Please follow me. We'll ask him when it will be ready."

Young van Horn followed the girl through a short, dark corridor pungent with herbs and spices. In a room behind the shop, a tall thin man stood grinding powders with a mortar and pestle. Young van Horn might have observed that the left sleeve of his garment was sewn up to the shoulder, empty. But he didn't. Perhaps he didn't notice because the man worked so skillfully, pausing now and then to add liquid from a flask, and some sweet-smelling, waxy stuff from a small crock on the table. Smoothly the man blended it all into a thick paste. While the man worked, the girl explained van Horn's request. She was blushing.

"There," said the thin man. "The salve must rest for three days. Then you may take some for your father." He looked up from the worktable. "I am Justin Carver, and this is my daughter and apprentice, October."

"Van Horn," stammered van Horn. It took all of his will to look away from the girl and into the kind eyes of Justin Carver. All van Horn could think was, October, October. What a perfect name! and similar things, for the poor young man was completely gone, deep in love. The girl, plain to see, was in the same state. Patiently, Master Carver directed his daughter to close the shop, and young van Horn to stable his horse. Then he invited young van Horn to accompany them home, where they could have some supper and talk.

The walk through the garden to Master Carver's house

went slowly, but not one of them seemed to mind. Young van Horn might have noticed that Master Carver walked somewhat awkwardly, for Carver had one wooden leg, but he didn't. Young van Horn's eyes and ears were for October.

Once inside the house, Master Carver ordered supper, which was marked by long looks and equally long silences on the parts of young van Horn and October. Nevertheless, by the end of the evening Master Carver seemed satisfied with the replies the young man had made to his patient questions. Carver, too, had been guilty of some long silences, during which he had stared at a peculiar ornament on the mantlepiece, an odd mug, with a twisted, sad face and drooping ears for handles.

After the servant had shown young van Horn to his room, and October had retired to hers, Master Carver sat alone in front of the fire. When his pipe was done, he stood up and knocked the ashes onto the grate. Putting away his pipe, he carefully picked up the ugly mug. Whispering softly into one of its great ears, Carver took the mug out of the room. The ugly mug, which van Horn had dreamed held all his happiness, the mug he'd searched for but not found, would be a perfect wedding gift.

THE PERFECT
SOLUTION

Ohhh, Jonah! His passion was fishing, and he had the luck that fishermen sometimes have. Sometimes he caught big fish, and sometimes small, and sometimes his lures or hooks got caught in weeds underwater, and sometimes they snagged in trees.

There were times when hooks snapped back. There could be as many as three barbed hooks on a beautiful lure that looked just like a tiny little silver fish. There were times when those hooks snagged underwater. Jonah then gave an expert tug, and the hooks snapped back toward that fisherman named Jonah and caught, one, two, three, in his sweatshirt.

And when those hooks were truly and well caught in his sweatshirt, that dedicated fisherman named Jonah used the scissors on his sweatshirt. After all, what serious fisherman would casually destroy a good lure?

Perhaps if Jonah had been older, the results would have been different, but as it was he was a boy, small for his age, even though everyone acknowledged that he was a skilled and exceptionally fortunate fisherman.

It happened to Jonah that he fished one year during a particularly bad time. It was a summer to remember, an impossibly cold, rainy summer, with nasty gusts of wind over the water where Jonah fished. In such weather Jonah needed a sweatshirt for warmth. He changed his sweatshirts several times every day because the shirts invariably got damp. And, in the gusty winds that summer, hooks were snagging right, left, and center, so that Jonah used the scissors on his sweatshirts rather often.

All too soon Jonah's mother held up one sweatshirt after another for Jonah's inspection.

"Jonah! Just look!"

Jonah looked.

"What have you done?!"

Jonah shrugged.

"Jonaaaaahhhh!" his mother cried in despair.

But Jonah was gone, gone fishing.

The cold and rain continued. Jonah's mother's grumbling continued, and Jonah's use of the scissors continued.

For a while, Jonah's big sister merely listened, once even tried to remove some barbed hooks from one of Jonah's sweatshirts without recourse to the scissors.

She failed.

Then Jonah's big sister retired to her chemistry lab out back in the shed, emerging from it only when she could announce, triumphantly, that she had the solution. In her test tube was the liquid necessary to make all of Jonah's sweatshirts self-healing!

One by one every single sweatshirt Jonah possessed was soaked in that solution, and then the whole sodden mess was dried in the huge tumbling dryers in the village laundromat. From that day on, the ragged edges of every cut, every tear, every ripped seam of Jonah's sweatshirts grew seamlessly back together within minutes. A large cut or tear took hours to grow back together until the cloth was perfect again.

The formula was perfect, and for a time Jonah's life was also perfect. The fish were biting, big ones, perfect for dinner. Sure, hooks still got caught, and Jonah still used the scissors, but the sweatshirts healed, and Jonah's mother smiled at fish, shirts, and boy.

Alas, Jonah's life might have remained perfect if Jonah had stuck to fishing and ignored the latest fashions.

But, as it was, Jonah, who was small for his age, had grown a bit bigger that wet summer. He complained one evening that the sleeves of a favorite old sweatshirt were now too short and the neck too tight. Because it was the fashion, no one thought a thing about it when Jonah cut out the sleeves of his old sweatshirt. He then cut the neck hole bigger, and then cut off the slightly stretched cuff at the bottom of that sweatshirt. When he was finished, Jonah put on the sweatshirt. Jonah looked in that sweatshirt just like all the other kids in their cutout sweatshirts, except of course that Jonah was small for his age. And no one thought a thing about it when Jonah wore that sweatshirt to sleep because all the kids did that, too.

It took all night for the perfect solution to heal the cuts in that sweatshirt. It took all night for the sleeves of that cut-out sweatshirt to grow and grow and grow. All night, while Jonah slept, the cutout neck of his sweatshirt grew and grew and grew. The cutout hem of Jonah's sweatshirt grew that night while Jonah lay curled up asleep. That sweatshirt grew until it had healed itself completely shut.

With Jonah, who was small for his age . . . inside.

THE MIRROR

*F*or how many years had she been looking? Certainly ever since her mother first put together the costume, the first year of Woody. By now the gypsy-skirt had been lengthened; even so Shelley's ankles showed.

"It doesn't matter. I'll wear it," she'd replied when her mother puckered her brow and asked, "Shouldn't we find something else this Halloween?"

No. Nothing else. Of course she'd wear that costume. She'd walk out of the apartment door, go outside, where children swarmed over the lawns and sidewalks of the Elegant Garden Apartments. Shelley didn't ever actually join any group. She just made it seem that way until she was safely out of sight. Then Shelley always left the other children, left the Elegant Garden Apartments, and walked as far away as she could. Each year she went to a different group of houses. From door to door she went, "trick or treat," but had never yet found the door she meant to find.

Then, year after year, at the end of the night, Shelley dropped her bag of candy into the nearest trash can, and returned to the apartment. Woody would be mad. He always hoped she'd bring some candy he liked, but Shelley didn't go out for the candy and would not give him anything, not even a name.

She'd never once named him "Woody," not "my mother's friend," not "my mother's boyfriend," not "roommate," not "lover," nothing. For his part, Woody never beat Shelley, confining himself instead to the small pleasures derived by seeing her duck when he raised his fist or swung his palm as if to hit her. Much as she hated herself for it, Shelley never could stop that cringing. For Woody, the second little pleasure was to bellow out the shortened version of his nickname for Shelley. "Jack! Jack!" he'd call out over the lawns of the Elegant Garden Apartments whenever he had the slightest pretext for calling her. She never knew just when he'd decide to say the whole word to the whole neighborhood.

If Shelley did come home late, she'd find that Woody, in a great show of helpful domesticity, had set the table. At Shelley's place he'd put the largest serving utensils, or some bent or broken thing he'd brought just for the occasion. "There you are, Jackass," he'd say. "Your place, the special Jackass place just for you."

How she hated him. Back then, when he had first moved in, Shelley had been just a little kid, with nowhere for her hatred to go. She'd drawn Woody's picture again and again, then stabbed the pages full of holes with her pencil.

Nowadays she concentrated entirely on keeping out of his way. "Understand all; forgive all," said one of the proverbs in her French book, but Shelley couldn't. Her mother hinted that Woody had suffered in his childhood. "He's jealous of you; that's all," she'd once said, as if one sentence explained how a man of thirty could be jealous of a girl of twelve. It didn't work for Shelley, but then her only knowledge of men came from books, and Shelley was careful to read only those in which the fathers and daughters were best friends, or ones in which benevolent families were present in some dim background while the stalwart heroine triumphed in chilling adventures. These books she read mostly in the garages of the Elegant Garden Apartments, though hiding there had disadvantages. More than once she had seen or heard things she was not meant to observe, which left her feeling guilty, dirty, and miserable. In the apartment Shelley read in the closet of her room, by flashlight, with the door closed. Woody still had not discovered her there.

One of the many satisfactions of the costume was that Woody hated it.

"Why that kid wants to be a filthy, stinking gypsy is beyond me!" he had raged just last year at Shelley's mother when she had taken the package from the back of the linen closet. Shelley had unfolded the skirt, which had been made from an old drape. It was satisfyingly faded, a yellow-beige, with huge cabbage roses on it, and the ruffle on the bottom a bit stained from where it had dragged on the ground when she was smaller. The big black beads lay under the skirt.

Once that long strand had gone four times around Shelley's neck and still hung down to her waist. This year she'd be able simply to put it on and let the beads swing nearly to her knees. The shawl, good for cold nights, shimmered in two colors, and the headscarf was pure silk, in shades of purple. And, finally, there was the blouse, of fine white batiste, so thin you could read through it. The blouse came from some time in her mother's past, when there had been parents and grandparents and servants and trips to Europe, and that blouse, with its embroidery and its many tucks, belonged to that time. There was also one earring, gold with black enamel. "Spanish," her mother had said, "the last of a pair."

For Shelley, last year was gone, but in a few hours they'd take the costume down, and she'd wear it again, and this year surely she'd find the right door.

So far she had done everything to make the evening go as

smoothly as possible. Straight from school she had come home, not to read, but to make the dinner, set the table, even clean the bathroom. Of course, nothing she did could prevent Woody's complaining that her meals tasted terrible, but at least dinner would be over early.

"Oh, oh, Jackass. Halloween again." He leered, his big death's head tall above her. Shelley ducked, went into the kitchen to help her mother carry the food to the table.

"We won't be home when you finish your trick or treating," her mother said. "The Winslows are having a grownup party."

Shelley nodded. They sat down.

Tonight Woody played a different game. All through dinner he smiled and bobbed, praising every dish fulsomely, helping himself to miniscule second and third portions, dragging out the meal to make her cry. Sometimes, too often, he succeeded. But tonight Shelley refused to show impatience. She'd wait until he tired of his game.

Just as Woody seemed about to take a fourth helping, her mother glanced at the clock, "Oh, time to change. Shelley, you clear." Woody tipped back his chair and watched her take away the dishes, humming cheerfully to himself. Finally she was done.

Shelley washed and dried her hands, put away the towel, and walked to the linen closet. She opened the door and reached to the back of the shelf for the costume. It wasn't there.

"Mother. Did you take out my costume already?" Shelley worked very hard to keep her voice calm, level, no hint of what she felt. Woody, humming in the kitchen, was so happy.

"No. I didn't," came her mother's voice from the bedroom.

"It's gone."

"That's impossible. I haven't changed anything in that closet." Her mother, wearing only underwear, came out into the hall, touched the neat stacks of sheets and towels on the shelves before she turned to look for Woody. He had, meanwhile, walked casually to the living room and picked up the newspaper.

"Woody?" her mother began.

"She's too old for that gypsy crap." He snapped the newspaper open in front of his face.

"But Woody," her mother began, "those things were mine . . . and. . . ."

She started toward him, but Shelley touched her arm. Putting a finger to her lips, Shelley shook her head at her mother. He wanted them to cry, to beg. Shelley had seen it before. This time she wouldn't let her mother beg.

"It's no problem. No problem at all. I've got another costume. See you later." She forced a grin at her mother, then ran into her room and grabbed the top sheet from her bed. The costume had mattered, mattered too much, more than anything, but not now. Now she'd find the door without it, tonight.

Shelley wrapped the sheet around herself, took up her shopping bag and ran out the back door. "Have a good party!" She was gone.

Away from the Elegant Garden Apartments she ran. The sheet, part toga, part sari, part winding sheet, flapped around her. She ran as fast as she could so that the costume could not matter.

After she had reached an unfamiliar neighborhood, she stopped running and looked around. "Let this be the street!" she whispered fiercely, and strode up to ring the first bell. "Trick or treat!" What a cheerful, musical voice she could produce. It wasn't the right house, so Shelley tried another one. Hours later, nearly time to return home,

Shelley rang one last bell. The man who opened the door peered out at her through the screen door. He was drunk. "Aren't you a pretty thing," he croaked. "Here, come inside and let's get a look at your costume." Before the door could open, Shelley was gone. But she couldn't stop on bad luck. Never. That decided her; she'd try one, two, three more.

When the third door opened, Shelley sighed. An old woman, dressed exactly as Shelley should have been dressed, even to the single Spanish gold earring, smiled at her and hugged her close. "We've been waiting."

"It took so long," Shelley sighed again. "Strange." She took another deep breath. "I smell cloves."

The old woman laughed. "I always suck on one. It reminds me to think before I speak." She held Shelley out to look at her. "You are finally here." And as Shelley looked back into the old woman's face, it shimmered and changed until it was Shelley's own face. It was her face on her body that looked back, gasped when she gasped, laughed when she laughed, but then said, "Come."

Shelley stepped across the threshold onto springy grass and followed the Shelley she saw in front of her into a grove of trees where wagons stood in a circle around a fire. Beyond the trees horses grazed near the arches of an aqueduct; nearby, the ruins of a fountain spewed water into a cracked basin. At the fire people sat, with children on laps, babies curled up asleep, small children sitting wide awake, listening.

"The children of the people are never put to bed," the other Shelley said.. "By listening all their lives to the stories, they know them and learn to tell their own. You'll be safe here." She smiled, turned away and then turned back, "And one thing more, a piece of advice . . . A gypsy girl will never find a husband unless she is skilled at begging from strangers." Shelley repeated, "From strangers."

Shelley settled herself, tucked the gypsy-skirts around her bare feet, at what she knew was her own place by the fire. There she would sit for the rest of the telling. Twice at least before she slept, she thought how good it was that the stories would be told night after night, again and again until she knew them all. When she awoke, the other Shelley was gone.

Woody pretended not to be at all surprised to see the gypsy costume. He claimed aloud, and no one contradicted him, that he had given it back to Shelley after all. Just a little joke, but after that night he did say more than once how glad he'd be when that kid was grown and gone. "She gets weirder and weirder with those old woman eyes. How come she smells like cloves, and never says a word?"

THREE GRAINS
OF RICE:
FROM THE BONES OF AN
ARAB FOLKTALE

The figs were ripe. Soon they'd be picked, then put out in the sun to dry, then threaded on strong twine, and tied up in neat bunches to keep for the winter. Fish, crusted with salt, already lay drying in the hot, bright light that filled the days.

In just a few weeks, Timoor and Beyah would be married and live the rest of their lives in the rocky village carved into the cliffs that rose straight out of the blue sea. Every morning Beyah led the goats from the village up the dusty path to the stony meadows. There she sewed while she watched the goats feeding on the grass and wildflowers. No girl in the village wove better cloth, nor sewed a neater seam. Not one had a stronger arm with a rock, nor deadlier aim when any predator came near the goats, than did Beyah, Beyah of the mischievous black eyes.

Timoor adored her.

The wedding shirt for Timoor was long finished, the softest, strongest, most beautiful shirt ever made for a bridegroom by a bride in that village. Beyah's own dress, too, was ready, waiting for the day.

But the wedding day never came. Two neighboring countries were at war with one another. Quite by accident a skirmish took place outside the village, an unfortunate accident. Afterward, the goats were scattered and Beyah lay dead, just one small mark on her right temple. The long, bright scarf that once covered her hair had slipped off her head, allowing the wind to blow the fine black strands across her lips.

Timoor found her there, carried her to the village, straight to the door of old Loma. The whole village knew that Loma could brew a potion to set love aflame, another that would calm a baby's cough, still another to cause an enemy's undoing, another to cure warts. Everyone knew Loma was powerful enough to bring back the dead. Everyone knew.

"Auntie Loma," Timoor whispered outside her door, "Auntie Loma, please let me in."

The door opened. Without a word, the old woman led the boy inside. Gently, he put the still body of Beyah on the old woman's bed. Timoor knelt on the earthen floor beside her.

"Please, please, Auntie Loma, bring her back to life," sobbed Timoor.

"You have always been a good boy, Timoor," Loma replied. "You have always been both gentle and generous, and I will give you what I can."

"You will?" Timoor looked up.

"If I can lay upon her lips three little grains of rice." Hearing the old woman's cracked whisper, Timoor's face brightened with hope.

". . . three grains of rice that have been cooked in a pot that has never been used to cook a meal in sorrow."

"Just three grains?! Of course! I'll go! I'll go right now!"

Timoor jumped up and kissed the old woman on the top of her head, then ran out the door.

First he raced to Rengi's, surely the happiest house in all the village. Rengi's house was always full of laughter. Rengi would lend him the pot. Breathless, Timoor arrived at her door, where he was greeted with shouts, giggles and hugs by the children tumbling about. After sending one child to call for their mother, Timoor restlessly waited for her to appear. "Dear Rengi," he began, "I've come, please, dear Rengi, to borrow a pot for cooking rice, a pot that's never been used to cook a meal in sorrow."

Rengi's smile faded. "Ah, Timoor, gladly I'd lend you any pot, but this one was used when my own father died, and this when . . ." She shook her head.

From door to door Timoor went through the village . . . No one refused. He could borrow any pot in the village, from the most battered and scorched to the finest of all . . . but . . . "in this we made the food when my firstborn lay sick, my firstborn who will never be well" . . . "Ahh, Timoor. We have used this pot when Kalash went away" . . . "and this pot we used at the time my son's boat was lost" . . . at every doorway there was a pot and with every pot a story. When he returned to Loma's house, Timoor saw that the old woman had washed Beyah, dressed her in the wedding dress, and combed smooth that long black hair.

"I understand," he said.

With his own hands Timoor prepared a place in the stone caverns of the dead in the cliff that rose straight up from the blue sea.

PROSPERITY

An orphaned boy stood by the side of a road, waiting. He had chosen a spot at the crest of a hill. From where he stood, concealed by tall weeds, he could see far down the road in both directions. Because of the hill, any approaching wagon would be going quite slowly by the time it reached him.

As the hours passed, the boy could hear, as well as feel, the rumbling of his empty stomach. Otherwise, the only sounds were the rasp of the insects and the rattle of the wind pushing dry seed pods one against the other.

No wagons came. The sun set; the evening breeze made the boy's skin prickle with cold. An hour after moonrise, he heard a wagon in the distance, then saw the lean old horse, milk-white in the moonlight, struggle up the hill.

The boy crouched down in the weeds. He recognized neither horse nor wagon, but he'd need to see the driver first, before he dared to speak.

At the crest of the hill, the wagon slowed, stopped. The driver, hunched on the wagon seat, turned his face toward the boy. He was very old, his face ashen in the moonlight. "Want a ride, boy? You running away?"

"Only from the orphanage." The boy straightened up, taller than the weeds. "They don't really care." He took one step forward. "How'd you know I was here?"

"Horse smelled you, and now we can both hear your stomach. Climb up. There's stew in the pot, still warm."

"Thank you, sir." The boy climbed into the wagon bed, and found the battered pot. Sitting crosslegged with the stewpot in his lap, he took his spoon from his pocket and ate, chewing every bite for a very long time. Who knew when he'd eat again?

Meanwhile, without a word from the old man, the horse resumed his slow pace. After a time, the boy stopped eating, not wanting to make the old man angry at him for being greedy. The boy felt almost satisfied, and hardly seemed to have made any difference in the level of stew in the pot, so probably he'd quit eating in time. The wagon creaked on through the deserted countryside, through moonshadow and moonlight. Carefully returning the stewpot to its place, the boy climbed up onto the wagon seat beside the old man, who mumbled something.

"Pardon, sir?" the boy asked.

"My turn," said the old man.

Perplexed by the old man's response, the boy was silent for a while, and then asked.

"Where you headed?"

"The town the foreigners made, the one they called 'Prosperity,'" the old man answered.

"Prosperity?" the boy repeated, a bit disappointed. He'd hoped to go somewhat farther away from the orphanage, even though they'd hardly look for him in Prosperity. No one went there, ever. "The ghost town?"

The old man nodded. "It's my turn."

"Turn to do what?" the boy ventured.

"When the foreigners dug a mine there, and built a railroad there, in the most sacred place in all the world, they made a great tear in the fabric of time. They disturbed the peace of many souls. I help to mend it."

"Help? How do you know what to do?"

"The spirits from the other side instruct us. My brother's service ends tonight. It is my turn." He gestured toward the wagon bed. "You sleep now. I'll awaken you when we arrive."

The boy wanted to hear more, and was not at all sure he wanted to sleep, not so sure he wanted to close his eyes while they approached souls not at peace, but the old man's tone left no room for argument, and the boy did feel all the accumulated tiredness of that whole, long day. Back he crawled, pulled on a scratchy wool blanket that smelled of horse, and was instantly asleep.

When he awoke, the moon was gone, the night dark and utterly silent. The horse had been unhitched from the wagon, and stood freshly groomed, pale and shimmering, as if from his own light.

The old man stood by the horse's head, stroking the animal and whispering.

The boy strained his ears to hear.

"My turn," the old man said.

Sitting up, the boy folded the blanket, stretched, and climbed down from the wagon. Where would he go now? Into the ghost town that lay just beyond the forest? No. He'd walk back a mile or so to the crossroads, hope he'd find another ride, then a place where he could work.

"Here." The old man held out the reins toward the boy. Not understanding, the boy kept his hands at his sides. "Take them," the old man ordered. "Take the horse. He appears to be old to avoid exciting the envy of those who would steal him, but he never tires. Take the wagon and the stewpot. It is never empty. Go, and come back here to return them to me in seven years."

"Seven years?"

"Yes. In seven years." With that the old man stepped into the forest and was gone.

With a shudder, the boy hitched the horse to the wagon, climbed up and started off, back to the crossroads. Once there, he watered the horse at a nearby stream, and then continued on his way.

Seven years? The old man would most likely be dead in seven years, the horse for sure in less. Seven years? And the stewpot? Tying the reins loosely, the boy climbed back into the wagon, then returned to his seat with the stewpot in his arms. To his surprise, the stew was still warm, and tasted even better than before. One spoonful followed another into his mouth as the wagon rumbled slowly along. The boy filled his stomach until it hurt. The level of stew in the pot did not change.

And so the seven years passed. The boy grew up, with horse and wagon to help him earn his way, and always enough to eat. He lived with a comfort and freedom he'd only dreamed.

At the end of the seven years, the horse, of his own accord, turned his head toward the ghost town called Prosperity. The boy had often debated with himself whether or not he'd return. He hadn't actually promised, after all. But the horse and the stewpot had served him well for seven years, until he was grown and strong. He could have let the horse go alone, but he didn't. He'd take them back and say his thank you.

It was long after the moon had set when the horse stopped beside the dark wood. The boy unharnessed the horse, rubbed him till his coat glittered in the night with a light all its own.

Abruptly the old man stood there beside him, looking not one minute older than when they had parted. Before the boy could speak, the old man clasped him firmly by the shoulders, turned him toward the forest that led to Prosperity, and in a tone that left no room for argument, said, "Your turn."

Second Dream

CARLO THE SILENT

He was, in every other way, a perfect baby. When he was born, his mother and father had touched each perfect tiny nail on each perfect finger and toe. As the days, weeks, and months passed, they watched him grow. His eyes, which were large and luminous, looked at the world with understanding, humor, and compassion. He could hear—they were certain of that—and he showed them he knew the names of things. As a small child, he loved noise as much as any little boy: firecrackers, doors slamming, thunder, and rain on the summer garden.

With all of that, not a sound, not even a sigh was ever heard from Carlo's lips. Never, that is, until the night, just two days after Carlo's sixth birthday, when Uncle Fred tried to help.

Uncle Fred and Carlo were hiking when they missed the path. It got dark and late, and they were far from the spot where they had planned to camp. After sunset the wind came up cold and sharp, bringing little flurries of snow. They found a shallow hollow in the mountainside, not nearly big enough to call a cave, and put down their packs. The dinner they ate was cold, and a little dry: They were short of water so couldn't make anything better. Uncle Fred tried to be his usual cheerful, hearty self, but the rocks nudged him through his sleeping bag, and he had a raw blister on his left foot, so he gave up talking and suggested they go to sleep

Carlo slept.

Uncle Fred scratched his whiskers, wished he had a smoke, and listened to the wind, which seemed to be trying to take the mountain apart stone by stone. He must have dozed, for it was midnight when Uncle Fred, cold, stiff, and thirsty, woke up. Clouds scudding across the moon released light upon the mountain in unnerving fits and starts. Uncle Fred closed his eyes, but could not sleep.

Attempting to ease his cramped muscles, he sat up slowly. Catching sight of Carlo, Uncle Fred smiled in disbelief. "Just look at him. He's comfortable, sleeping like a baby, smiling at his dream. At that dream . . . Just look at what that boy is dreaming!"

Uncle Fred inched closer. To keep the dream from noticing him, from escaping, Uncle Fred concentrated hard on his own left ear. Closer, closer, closer.

There! He had it! In his hands was a slippery old trout of a dream.

"Haha!" Uncle Fred cackled joyfully. "While I've had rocks in my spine, the boy's been dreaming of fishing."

Uncle Fred kept a firm grip as the powerful old trout twisted and turned in his hands.

"Let me go!" it burbled.

"Not so fast," replied Uncle Fred. "This boy needs a blessing, but I have to think hard so I get him the best deal I can . . . Let's see . . . he needs to be able to speak, and . . ."

"Agreed," said the trout.

"Not so fast!" said Uncle Fred. "Being able to speak is not a proper blessing, more of a necessity. He needs a real blessing. He's my nephew after all . . . something like . . . Let me see."

Uncle Fred thought hard. He knew himself to be a blustering man, full of opinions, and he felt himself a man who should have been rich and thereby "successful" in the eyes of the world. But he wasn't rich. He wanted the power of speech for Carlo, and the power of wealth as well. To Uncle Fred respected meant rich in money.

During all the time it took for Uncle Fred to think, the trout never ceased struggling. Uncle Fred was sweating by the time he finally had his wish right in his head and began to speak. "Now trout. Give him this . . . Prosper. Yes. Everything Carlo does must prosper, thrive. I want the boy to succeed after all."

"Agreed," replied the trout. "Now let go!"

"Okeydokey," chortled Uncle Fred.

"Just one thing more," said the trout.

"What's that?" asked Uncle Fred.

"The boy can speak, and everything he does will prosper—for others!"

"No, no, no. Wait a darn minute," shouted Uncle Fred. "I was just trying to do the boy a favor! I was not greedy! Be reasonable!"

The trout was gone.

Carlo laughed out loud in his sleep, and Uncle Fred slid, unconscious—just as if someone had rapped him on the head—slid deeply asleep, deep into his sleeping bag.

They awoke the next morning with dew on their faces.

"Uh, Carlo," said Uncle Fred, long after breakfast, long after they had rechecked their map and started back to find the trail they'd missed. "Uh, Carlo. I have some good news and some bad news for you."

Carlo looked interested but did not speak.

"You. You can talk now." Uncle Fred grinned encouragingly at Carlo. When Carlo remained silent, he nodded and smiled, urging Carlo to reply. The boy didn't seem particularly interested in trying.

"Well then," said Uncle Fred. "Let me tell you what happened last night," and he did.

When he had finished his story, Uncle Fred looked once again, quite intensely, at Carlo. "You're not mad with me, are you?"

Carlo shook his head.

"You won't speak?" whispered Uncle Fred.

"Sometimes," said Carlo softly.

"Oh," grunted Uncle Fred. "Uhh . . . sometimes." He attempted a grin. "I understand." But he didn't.

From that time on Carlo could speak, though he rarely chose to do so. As people grew to know him, they became comfortable with him and his silence. Everything the trout had said proved true. Whatever Carlo did prospered, and *how* it prospered! . . . for others.

When, as a very young man, Carlo went out in the world to make his living, he began by taking Uncle Fred's most frequently repeated advice. In spite of Carlo's own preference, which was to be out-of-doors, Carlo went into the tumultous indoor world of high finance. In no time at all, he made great, huge, staggering amounts of money . . . for others.

It had seemed logical to Uncle Fred when he suggested banking that Carlo would make money for others, who would then be grateful and reward Carlo so that he could live comfortably. Uncle Fred had thought long and hard about that mixed blessing he had obtained for Carlo, tried to make it satisfy his own waking dream of success for his nephew. It did not work. The more money Carlo made for others, the less others rewarded him.

Carlo left banking.

For the next few lonely years, he wandered around the

world, doing this and that, never finding a way to live with the blessing Uncle Fred had secured for him. For himself, Carlo could not even boil water.

Discouraged, Carlo returned to his homeland.

After a few days, he hiked back up the long path to the hollowed-out place on the side of the mountain where he and Uncle Fred had slept. Carlo hoped to dream of the trout, and to give the blessing back.

Late that night Carlo sat listening to the wind as it tried to take the mountain apart stone by stone. As he listened, with his back comfortably leaning against one boulder and his feet resting on another, Carlo heard the answer, and when he heard it, Carlo laughed out loud. The echo of his laugh, as it boomed back and forth among the mountain tops, sounded so much like the voice of Uncle Fred that Carlo had to laugh once again. At last Carlo knew how to live with the blessing Uncle Fred had secured for him.

The next morning Carlo returned to the world and set to work with joy.

The answer that Carlo heard and understood was one that bewildered the rest of the world.

Listen. Hear them whisper. Ah, they say, Silent Carlo. What a peculiar, taciturn young man. Isn't he odd to live in such a bare stone house, behind a plain stone wall? And look inside the garden wall: What is that? Sand, sand on the earth and five boulders, boulders rising out of the sand.

Ah, Carlo the Silent, they say. He has planned and planted the most varied, the most loved gardens in the world, gardens that flourish, that delight the soul . . .

How is it that he, the master gardener, lives peacefully without so much as a blade of grass?

HEDWIG THE WISE

In January, Hedwig, queen of the Eastern Kingdom, was strong, beautiful, wise, and kind, and she was a happy woman. Beside her she had a beloved husband, Bergen, king of the Western Kingdom, and together they watched with joy as their two children grew. The children, a girl and a boy, cared very much for one another, but indeed were spirited, so that sometimes the queen did say, "Children. If you must quarrel, please take yourselves outside, or to a wing of the castle rather far from here. I cannot hear myself think."

That was in January.

By spring, when all the earth had awakened from winter's harsh sleep and was bursting forth into bloom, King Bergen was dead.

That was spring.

Queen Hedwig was still deep in mourning that fall when Princess Gabriella, who had gone down to the harbor to watch the ships, disappeared without a trace.

The queen's grief was so overwhelming that she could not look upon her son without weeping, fearful that at that very moment he, too, would be taken from her.

The boy, unable to bear his mother's sorrow, finally resolved to find his sister, and set sail one morning with the tide. No sooner had he left the harbor than he was taken up by a most terrible storm. Day and night his little boat was buffeted by wind and wave, shaken by thunder, and the mast split by lightning. When finally the sea became calm, the boy had lost all idea of where he could be or for how long he had traveled. After a time, he beached his tiny craft on a rocky and desolate shore.

Quite shaky for lack of his land legs, the prince climbed out of his boat and started inland. He had not gone very far when he saw in the distance a girl kneeling by a pond that lay in a hollow of the rocky landscape.

"Good day, beautiful maiden!" he greeted her. "What brings you to this desolate place?"

"Good morning, handsome youth!" the girl replied. "I am here because the giant who rules this land kidnapped me. Because I refuse to marry him, he compels me to wash his dirty socks here in this pond." She stood up, dried her hands on her apron, asking, "And who are you?"

"Victor Phillip Charles Frederick Bergen Andrew, Prince of the Western Kingdom." He bowed deeply as he spoke. "At your service. I am here searching for my sister, who has disappeared from our homeland."

As he spoke, the girl began to smile and then to laugh.

"Vico! You forgot to include your baptismal names. Albert Alfred Robert Roland." She moved toward him as if she would give him a great hug, as they used to do when they were children, but, suddenly shy, she stopped and made a deep curtsey.

The prince looked stunned.

"I," said the girl, "am Princess Gabriella, your big sister, and I shall NOT give all the rest of my names."

With that they did embrace, and immediately sat down on the boulders on the edge of the pond to talk over all that had happened.

After a time, the air grew rapidly colder. Princess Gabriella shivered. "The giant will be home soon."

"Then let's leave now. My boat is still seaworthy," her brother urged.

"No. He'd catch us before we were out of the cove. No. We can't run away. We are trapped here. A human can leave this land only if carried from here by the giant himself." She stared out over the water for quite a long time before she once again shivered with the cold, and then spoke. "We'll return to his castle and I'll think of a plan."

In silence they trudged along, bearing the basket of wet socks between them.

As they walked, the rocks gave way to scattered trees, and gradually to forests and meadows rich with flowers. It was a wild countryside, but had a beauty the prince felt down to his bones.

At last, just as they reached the castle gate, the princess spoke. "I'm not certain yet what I'll do, but you must trust that whatever I say or do, I'll keep you safe and make certain our escape."

Prince Vico agreed, and they went into a side courtyard, where the prince and princess hung up the dripping socks. Afterward, they strolled about the main courtyard and entrance hall while Prince Vico asked about the statues, ornaments, and paintings that hung there.

After a short while, the earth trembled slightly beneath their feet. Gabriella went to the door, and shaded her eyes against the late afternoon sun. "Yes," she whispered. "I see him." She'd hardly spoken when the giant sang out, "Ohhhhh, beautiful princess. I smell the blood of humankind."

"Noooooh," sang the princess. "It is only IIIIII."

"Noooooohhh," sang the giant. "Like you but not you . . ."

"Good," sighed the girl, still whispering, "He's not in a

bad mood. Stand here, and greet him as you would a king. He is one even though I refuse him."

"Does he always sing?" whispered Vico. "His voice is rather nice."

"Always, or speaks in a very soft, low voice, or else we'd be destroyed by the sound," she replied.

"Good evening," said the princess cheerfully. "Look, here is my brother, Prince Vico of the Western Kingdom, come to pay us a visit."

Vico bowed low. The princess curtseyed with dignity and charm.

"Welcome to my home," sang the giant, returning the bow.

Gesturing that the prince and princess should precede him into the castle, the giant smiled broadly. "Yes, welcome, welcome to our guest. Princess, prepare a chest of gifts for our guest. He'll dine with me this evening, and then I myself will deliver your brother the prince to his doorstep, with treasures worthy of our royal visitor."

"Yes, of course," replied the princess, and smiled at the giant. "Of course." She embraced her brother. "I'll select the gifts. Farewell, dear brother. When I have packed your chest of treasures, I must prepare for my husband." And she smiled again at the giant, a smile so full of joy that the giant imagined that at last the princess would be his wife.

Prince Vico was surprised at his sister's words and manner, but remembered his promise to accept whatever she said or did. Hoping that she had indeed made a plan, he bade her farewell.

After Princess Gabriella had left the room, the giant called for food and drink, for music and dancing, and entertained Prince Vico until the boy's eyes blinked ever more slowly with tiredness.

While the giant and her brother were feasting and singing

together in the giant's great hall, the princess went to the giant's treasury, but instead of filling a chest, she emptied it. She then dragged the chest to a place near the door and attached a note: "For Prince Vico and Queen Hedwig from the Generous Giant." After that, she climbed inside and pulled closed the lid, locking the chest behind her.

It was near midnight when the giant picked up the drowsy boy and, taking the chest under his other arm, strode off into the moonlight, stopping only when he put boy and chest down on the front steps of Queen Hedwig's castle. The giant then returned home, where he discovered that Princess Gabriella had eluded him.

Queen Hedwig's sorrow fell away like an outgrown coat when she saw her children safely home.

For many weeks thereafter, friends, relatives, even strangers without number asked Princess Gabriella about the giant. Each and every time she replied, "He wasn't bad, for a giant. He had good manners, was musical, and an excellent storyteller. Nevertheless, I categorically refuse to be kidnapped into marriage!"

Before long Queen Hedwig, who had regained her strength and beauty, saw both her son and her daughter well married and each settled upon a throne, with babies shortly in the palaces of the Western and Eastern Kingdoms.

One evening King Vico and his queen and their baby and Queen Gabriella and her husband, who was king of the Southern Kingdom, and their baby all visited Queen Hedwig in her little summer palace, where she had invited them for coffee with whipped cream and little cakes.

The evening was gently warm, all the doors and windows open to the garden. The hours passed pleasantly in conversation, music, and games, not to mention the cakes and cream. Through it all Queen Hedwig had remained seated, summoning each of them, one by one, to her side for a little private chat. To each, and to every servant, she gave a precious gift, a painting, a jewel, a book, a musical instrument, until she had given away everything but what was packed in the trunks that stood in the room behind her. And when she was finished, she called all the assembled guests and servants to her.

"Mother?" Queen Gabriella and King Vico asked with alarm.

"Stop," commanded Queen Hedwig. "You are both hard at work and happy with your families . . ."

They both nodded agreement.

"But what are you going to do?" they asked.

"I," said Queen Hedwig, "am going to see the giant."

SAD EYES

My name means stranger in every language. It's my father's doing. Ever since I was a very young child, he has sent me alone, as his father sent him, to far-off lands to live and learn. He often says, "Men in our position must know all the world." He means that because of our enormous wealth we rule the world, and he believes first of all that we *can* know it and second that our knowledge will enable us to rule it well. But I think my father grew up reading too much Karl May, whose heroes are always greenhorns who prove themselves by doing extraordinary deeds in some exotic place. Frankly, I doubt many things. Nevertheless, I'm sure my father is the sort who could always be a hero. He's strong, clever, and charming. For me, these forced sojourns as a stranger in the world are mostly painful.

Japan began in the usual lonely way except that I was more a misfit than ever before. I am by nature an observer: elsewhere in the world I managed to be unobtrusive, to be a pair of eyes. In Japan I was an instant buffoon. I had become, in the course of the previous year, exceptionally tall, even for a European. Still, I have always tried to keep my body movements reserved, my voice low. In Japan, however, none of that mattered. Whatever I did, I was an awkward giant.

The first time I stepped aboard a bus, my head immediately became entangled in the advertising pennants strung just below the ceiling. Tiny fragile-looking old ladies stared and giggled, finally offering me the ultimate humiliation, that I, a hulking boy, should accept a seat from one of them.

The first meal I ate was alone in my hotel room, served by a girl little older than I, a girl whose English was only slightly better than my nonexistent Japanese. Throughout the meal I felt her eyes on me, felt certain she was barely suppressing laughter as I sat with my legs numb and chopsticks slipping.

Somewhere I had read that the Japanese eat chrysanthemum blossoms. Seeing a perfect yellow flower on one of the black lacquered plates, I asked the serving girl if one was supposed to eat it. She, smiling and bowing, said that if the gentleman wished to . . . and smiled again. I, blushing, put the flower in my pocket, muttering that I'd have it later. From that day on, out of my own curious perversity, I took back to my room every such flower that appeared on my plate, gradually amassing a collection of blooms whose beauty did not lessen as the petals dried.

Japan itself was disappointing. Streams and bays were choked with refuse. Tokyo was a grey, smoggy, ungraceful city. I was not totally ignorant of Japanese arts and crafts, and had expected their beauty to be everywhere evident. It wasn't. The country had all the ills of modern industrial society. There I was, under my father's orders. For weeks I followed guides through exquisite gardens, in and out of theaters, past works of art. Though everyone was courteous, those weeks made me long for places I'd been lonely in before. I yearned to be anywhere else.

Night after night I studied Japanese. Day after day I followed my guides. For the first time in my life I went everywhere with a guide. Otherwise the simplest task or journey could result in disaster.

Alone, foreigners who did not speak flawless Japanese were best advised to enter only those restaurants showing a willingness to serve foreigners by providing a window displaying plastic replicas of the food served, and prices given in Arabic numerals.

It was painfully clear that an unexpected foreigner was a burden to everyone. The only foreigner I met in those days, an American, told me that he regularly spoke Japanese on the telephone in the course of the business day. No problem. The minute he met people face to face they were so stunned to discover a foreigner that they refused to believe he spoke Japanese, and simply stared at him as if the dog were speaking. It was not an encouraging conversation.

I quickly learned that an accompanied foreigner was the responsibility of his host. A foreigner was like a madman or an animal in human garb, unpredictable; it may break all the Japanese rules of decorum, thereby humiliating itself and all who witness its acts. Such embarrassment was clearly to be avoided. Sensing the anxiety I aroused in the Japanese made me feel miserable and guilty.

Then I met Yamoda-san. His note, telephone call, and Yamoda-san himself all arrived within a space of three hours. He apologized for not calling on me sooner. He had been abroad on business, and had only just returned to Tokyo. He reminded me that we had met, when I was perhaps ten years old, in my father's office. For one brief second I wondered if my father, sensing my despair, had sent Yamoda-san, but I knew no one would ever tell me.

Dismissing all other guides, Yamoda-san took over my education. His small, dry hands steered his shiny little grey sedan through all the streets of Tokyo, and far into the back country. There were fresh flowers in a vase attached to the dashboard. Together with that kindly man in his seemingly endless wardrobe of grey suits, I took buses, trains, and subways. We visited gritty factories to do the morning exercises at 7 AM. At one of them we heard the speech of a young man who'd moved to Seattle as a child. There he had longed for his home in an isolated town at the tip of Japan. Now, back home in that town, he yearned for Seattle. The young man concluded by saying that he must cure himself of being an outsider. With all my heart I silently wished him luck.

As we traveled, I was amazed at how my Japanese was improving, though Yamoda-san and I spoke mostly in English.

I love to eat, and enjoyed all the meals Yamoda-san and I shared during those days, at sushi stall, noodle shop, or elegant restaurant, where I always pocketed whatever flower decorated my plate. Yamoda-san appeared not to notice.

There was something else he seemed not to notice, but whatever it was grew daily more present. At first I'd glimpse a hand or hear the quick intake of breath behind me. Because I tried so hard not to be noticed more than absolutely necessary, I'd steal a sideward glance to see if someone were there, and again to see if Yamoda-san showed any awareness of the presence. He never did, though it grew daily more persistent.

Yamoda-san, however, always looked at me with the same kind, patient, somewhat tired eyes. His expression hardly changed, even when he made the small, dry jokes I liked so much. He wasn't at all typical of the people we met every day, for most of them were quite expressive. In particular I remember one waiter who served us a "typical Japanese breakfast" of seaweed, rice, cold fish, and tea. I asked him what he usually ate for breakfast. "Eggs, over easy, with bacon, toast and orange juice," he replied. With a look of pained sympathy, he leaned over to whisper, "Japanese breakfast is simply dreadful!"

On the day we visited Nara, the weather turned cold. What sky we could see above the pines was bleak, lead-colored. Our talk there was of death. I began it, saying what I felt so strongly there, that it must be a spot favored by suicides.

"It disturbs you, too?" Yamoda-san replied. "For I especially feel their presence here."

"The suicides?" I asked. I could picture them quite vividly.

"Not only them," he sighed. "For not all suicides are restless spirits or unhappy dead. No. Here, especially, I feel the presence of the dead not at peace."

When I looked at him, his eyes were dull with sorrow. Perhaps he would have told me then, but I assumed he had a private trouble, and that I should spare his feelings. Clumsily, I turned away, suggesting we direct our walk out of the park. We did, three sets of footsteps echoing as we went. Yamoda-san seemed not to notice.

The next morning I received a note. Yamoda-san had abruptly been sent abroad on business. His note apologized, saying he had received the order too late to telephone my hotel, and suggesting I visit a certain textile museum while he was away. I didn't; I just buried myself in my room with my books and lived on crackers, fruit, and tea. When I did stick my nose out-of-doors, it was raining, which suited my mood perfectly. I returned to my books.

When Yamoda-san returned, nearly a week after our trip to Nara, he took me to the auditorium of an elementary school to hear a girl perform a traditional bride's song. Yamoda-san said she had won some prize and that she sang beautifully. The girl, her eyes and lips painted, her face white with rice powder, was wearing an elaborate head-dress and a bridal kimono from another time. She sang and danced so gracefully that I was half in love with her before she finished. The rest of the audience was wildly enthusi-astic, the girl charming.

Afterward, Yamoda-san introduced us. We talked for a while—I in my "improved" Japanese—when suddenly the girl began a most un-Japanese laugh. As she did, her whole posture was instantly Western. "I'm sorry," she said, in accents that were pleasantly American. "I was making little mistakes, more and more of them and I had to stop. For-give me, and after I change I'll treat you to some noodles." She bowed, once again Japanese, and was quickly gone, in that particular walk of Japanese women wearing a kimono.

I was offended that she and Yamoda-san had tricked me, but impressed at the girl's achievement. "She is extraordi-nary," said Yamoda-san. "When she performs, she is Jap-anese. Imagine. She's been here only one year." For a moment, I took his words as a reproach. Certainly, I could not pass for Japanese, but then that was never my father's purpose. And my purpose? I had been dutiful, but now I wanted very much to talk more with that girl. Yamoda-san excused himself saying he wanted to meet with some old friends and that I should come to such and such a place after the girl and I had consumed enough noodles.

We did consume noodles, and did talk in the most crowded noodle shop in all Japan. Talk! I was befuddled with joy at being with someone my own age, a girl full of plans and ideas, who also knew what it was to be in and of a place but also to be merely on its surface. I wanted to see her again and again, but she was leaving to attend univer-sity in the U.S.A.

At a certain point, the girl began to blush, and I realized

I'd been staring at her without speaking or eating. "Ah. Excuse me," I stammered, "but how many people are in this shop?"

The girl glanced at me speculatively, "Three: you, me, and the counterman. One person just left. Why?"

"I was hearing something, probably water in my ear from swimming, and I imagined it was people talking." I was impressed at how quickly I had come up with that explanation. The girl grinned. Nice grin. Embarrassed, I looked, trying to appear casual, around at the throng that pressed upon us. Only then did I comprehend that most of the crowd was incorporeal: spirits, presences, ghosts.

At least one of the ghosts belonged to the girl, I could tell, but whose were the rest?

As Yamoda-san and I drove home much later that night, I spent the better part of the journey thinking how to phrase my question. Nothing sounded correct, so I blurted it out, "Is that noodle shop known for its ghosts?"

"Ghosts? No. It couldn't survive if it had ghosts. Why?"

"The place was full of presences, spirits, ghosts. The one behind the girl was funny, more of a spirit. It kept lecturing her, 'Come home. Get married. Why on earth would a nice girl want to be a doctor of philosophy?'"

I laughed at the memory of its insistent pleading.

Yamoda-san stared ahead at the road without making any comment. When we said goodnight he seemed tired. I wondered if my ghost talk had offended him. Maybe he didn't believe me or thought I was trying to get back at him for having fooled me earlier. I resolved not to mention the subject again. Nor did I, even though something changed that night. From then on Yamoda-san and I were never alone: that presence I'd heard and felt before was always with us, heavy, insistent, pressing close. I could feel it whenever we were together. Yamoda-san, on contrast, seemed more distant. I worried that he had indeed been assigned to me and that he was thoroughly tired of the job. I tried to be cheerful, but blamed my father for his educational theories and wondered when I'd be allowed to leave Japan. Poor Yamoda-san looked quite beaten down when once again he was suddenly sent abroad for a few days.

He returned, looking somewhat better, and announced that I had earned a feast. He then took me for what I later realized was a sort of graduation ceremony, dinner in an exceptionally beautiful, traditional Japanese restaurant. No sign in any language marked its entrance. Inside we were met by Mama-san, the wife of the owner, who showed us to our private dining room. There we were served our meal in unhurried elegance. It was good, delicious in fact, and I was glad for my months of training because my long body sat in comfort through it all. Yamoda-san, too, seemed to enjoy himself, telling fortunes according to the ancient Chinese manner, first Mama-san's and then mine, both of them full of incredibly good fortune to come, with all misfortune safely in the past. It was a new talent of his. Mama-san seemed pleased with the bright future he saw for her, and politely praised my Japanese.

It was quite late by the time Mama-san had left us alone to talk over our final cup of tea. For one brief instant, I felt such comfortable well-being, like that split-second beautiful dream before you wake. Of course. Our evening had been so splendid exactly because we had lacked that heavy presence, and now it was back.

Such sudden despair settled on me that I trembled as if with cold. When I turned to look at Yamoda-san, his face was ashen with grief.

And then, slowly, the presence became fully visible. There between us sat a young man, barely older than I. In some ways he seemed even younger. Although he wore a kimono, he was not Japanese. He sat awkwardly, his hands clenched in his lap. As if under command, I was the first to speak. "You've been near us before." I hesitated. "I've felt you."

The boy looked only at Yamoda-san and did not answer.

"Yamoda-san," I said, "pardon me for asking. Do you know this presence?"

"Yes," he sighed. "I have tried many times to set his soul to rest, always without success. I have performed every rite, and I have tried to explain to him what happened whenever he comes to me in his anger and sorrow, but when I speak he seems not to understand me."

"Why does he come to you?"

"I was there that night . . . I was a little boy, living on our family farm, on another island. It was nearly the end of the Second World War. Late one night an American bomber crashed on the mountain, high above our village. We, the few old men and the young boys left in the village, we were the militia. We went up to the crash. Some of the Americans were alive. We took care of them until the authorities came to take them away. Some were dead. Those we buried. One, this boy . . ."

At this the boy shook with strong emotion, though he did not speak.

Yamoda-san continued. "This boy was badly injured. We could do nothing to help him. He was complaining . . . After some discussion, the leader of our group, who was the head of the militia, said that we should do the one honorable thing. And it was done, with all the proper ceremony, all performed absolutely correctly. It was done with honor. Afterward there was a proper burial. Years later the Americans came to take American bodies home to America. When they took up this boy's body and saw that he had been, as they called it, 'beheaded,' they were angry and demanded a trial of our militia leader. How could they fail to understand it was done for the boy's honor?"

During the telling, Yamoda-san had stared directly ahead as if he looked at a faraway place. Now he turned to me.

"Perhaps the boy has appeared now because he feels, as I do, that you can help us." Yamoda-san sighed. "Perhaps he will understand you."

Turning to the boy, I repeated the story as Yamoda-san had told it to me, as best I could. The boy spoke from within himself to me. He was sobbing. "I could see it all, from outside my body. I was watching. I couldn't understand what they said, but I could feel . . . feel . . . their feelings . . . fear . . . shame . . . Afterward I ran away. I hid myself. When I came back, I went to him, the youngest one there . . ."

The boy nodded toward Yamoda-san without taking his eyes from mine. "Maybe he could help . . . but no one could. They all thought I was a coward, complaining of pain, a baby!"

Tears ran down his face. He seemed ashamed, wiped them roughly away.

I touched his hand.

"No. No. I don't think so." I struggled for words. "For them, asking another to complete your death is a tradition. For them, death was preferable to dishonor, and they did fear that you, a foreigner, whom they did not understand, might dishonor himself. Yes, they could not bear to witness shame, for it shames the witness as well. They did what they did, the whole time putting themselves in your place, imagining what they themselves would want from others. They showed respect for you by the way they acted, with all the ritual they knew."

"They saw themselves in my place?"

"Yes."

For a long time we sat there, three still figures in that perfect little room.

The boy sighed. I could feel the release of pain in every part of his being.

For the first time, the boy and Yamoda-san looked at one another. Yamoda-san bowed, bowed low to the boy's ghost. The boy, awkwardly, but with obvious good intent, bowed still lower, then sat up and offered his hand.

Yamoda-san clasped it firmly for some time, and the boy was gone.

AT THE SIGN OF THE
BECKONING FINGER

"There is a collector for any single thing you can possibly name!" The antique dealer pronounced every word, slowly, with tremendous emphasis, ". . . and for some things you can't." She pushed with both hands against the hanging barn door, which creaked slowly open.

The dealer marched inside, adroitly making her way among the tables and benches. A boy, his first driver's license still crisp in the wallet that lay flat against his hip, peered in behind her, waiting.

"Here now!" she boomed. "Take this, for example, a set of shark's teeth. Belonged to an old recluse way back up in the mountains. The stains on them are blood . . . human."

The young man nodded appreciatively.

One by one the dealer turned on several lights, fly-specked bulbs that hung down on long, cobwebby electric wires strung from the rafters. Here and there she used the toe of her boot to switch on an electric heater, which immediately produced a strong odor of burning dust, but remarkably little heat, though the heater coils glowed bright orange in the gloom.

That same orange could be admired in the dealer's hair, which had been forced into coils and curls above her stern face, and then fixed there, apparently permanently. To keep that coiffure free of cobwebs, dust, or entanglement with the curious assortment of things that hung in the barn, she had developed a peculiar walk. Through the crowded barn she marched, stiff from the waist up, with her high shelf of a bosom thrust forward. By bending at the knees, she passed safely by or under one obstruction after another, talking all the while.

The young man who followed her into the barn was by contrast small and lank, with long, thin hands that hovered over the objects on the benches and tables as he timidly asked an occasional question of the dealer.

"And that jar near your left hand." She pointed to a cracked jar encrusted with filth. "Those are murderers' teeth, taken after executions. Collector went all over the world. Collected them and catalogued them, too."

The young man seemed preoccupied.

"You looking for something in particular?" To the unwary, that question, so casually asked, could mean a big difference in price.

"No . . . No . . ." the young man replied. "Just browsing."

"This here is. . . ." She rummaged in a box, picked out a rusty object and turned around. The young man was not in sight. The dealer peered right and left around the dusky barn, and, not seeing the young man, returned the rusty object to its box, grumbling. "Could have at least said 'thank you,' after I went to all the trouble to open up the whole place just for him. Browsing indeed!"

"This." The young man's voice came faint and cracked from the gloom at the far end of the room. He crouched beside a low table covered with plaster casts of footprints, of teeth and jaws, of palmprints and plants, animal tracks, and other odd objects, including a set of automobile tire tracks.

The dealer nodded her approval when she saw just

where the young man's slim hands hovered. "Oh, yes. Those. Those are casts of the tire tracks of old Mrs. Dingby's car."

The young man raised his eyebrows ever so slightly in an expression of mild interest, so she continued.

"Mr. and Mrs. Dingby lived on a farm, way out in the country. They got older and older and Mrs. Dingby was getting dottier and dottier, so when Mr. Dingby finally died she just left him where he was for some time, until the stench got to her. She was a tiny, old-fashioned farm woman, wore her hair in a little knot on the top of her head." The dealer shook her own flaming helmet slowly at the memory. The young man waited patiently, though it was bone-chilling cold in that barn.

"So one day when poor old man Dingby was pretty much an assault on her nose, she decided to take him away, but she didn't want to ruin the insides of her car, so she hitched him up with a rope tied to the bumper of the car, and in she got. She could barely see over the steering wheel, even with the help of the big cushion from the davenport, and off she drove, commencing to pull Mr. Dingby's corpse behind her. Well, sir, the rope was none too young itself, and broke, but she never saw, and drove on, and somewhere finally noticed or maybe even forgot why she went out at all and so drove home and had herself a cup of coffee.

"Somebody else found him and had no idea who it was, but they got the police, who followed the drag marks back to the house. She, old Mrs. Dingby, didn't much outlive him."

She paused. "Interested?" She inclined her head slightly toward the casts.

The young man's shrug was limp. He appeared to have transferred his attention to a hard, deeply cracked pair of leather ski boots. "Well," he drawled, "yesss, I might be . . . if . . . if the price is reasonable."

The dealer's irritated hiss produced a silver cloud in the cold air. "Reasonable! I'm always reasonable. Thirty's my price." She paused, judging the young man's interest and worth, "Thirty . . . for both casts." •

"I was thinking . . . ahhh." The young man never seemed younger nor more shy. "I was thinking that, say, . . . twenty."

"Wellll," drawled the dealer. "I'm a reasonable woman. Let's say twenty-five, meeting halfway so we both feel good."

The young man hesitated ever so slightly. "Hmmm . . . All right. Twenty-five."

Carefully he took out his very thin wallet and removed ever so slowly two tens and a five, which he gave to the dealer. Then, very slowly, he picked up the plaster casts.

"Anything else today?"

"No, thank you." The young man cradled the plaster casts tenderly in his arms. He had reached the barn door before he turned around to look at her, revealing a smile of purest bliss, the smile of the collector rewarded. He spoke softly, his tone hushed, each word clear. "No, thank you. I've already got the rope, the cushion, the car, and the remains."

Third Dream

THE PRICE OF MAGIC

ob seized the nightmare by one violently kicking hind leg. Sinewy and covered by coarse hair, it seemed to be that of a goat. Rob held tight, though something warm and sticky oozed from the leg. Blood? The smell was dreadful. Rob managed to sit up in bed, still clinging to the struggling creature.

"It's true you know!" The nightmare hissed at him, its eyes glaring yellow in the darkness. Rob held tight.

"What's true?" Rob tried hard to see the creature's face in the writhing mass of legs and horns.

"All I've been telling you. It's all true. You are the baby in that nightmare! Only I can help you escape." The creature panted loudly in the darkness. "But first let go!"

"Swear," Rob demanded.

"I swear. Now let go!"

Rob released his grip on the creature's leg. Something foul remained on his hand.

"Here. Let me take that away," soothed the creature. "Repeat after me, 'I wish that this zotum be gone from my hand.'"

Rob obeyed. Before the words were out, Rob choked and gagged uncontrollably. The smell had become, if possible, even more overpowering. His hand was clean; his *chest*, warm and sticky. "*I* could have wiped it on myself!" Rob whispered furiously, suddenly aware that their struggle might awaken his mother.

"Sorry. I didn't intend for it to go there. Try again. Say you wish the zotum would be out in the swamp behind your house, smeared on a tree."

Rob made the wish. The stuff was gone.

"Now," sighed the creature, "that's better. Now we can talk sensibly. There are important things you must know. Your dream is true. Your mother was once a powerful enchantress. She wanted a child, you, and wanted you all to herself alone. To keep you from the world, she went off to a most secret, hidden spot for your birth. After you were born, she wove a web of magic all around you, magic so strong that she was left weak, a mere mortal. But you, you are trapped. She has made you a child forever!"

"Forever?" echoed Rob.

"Until . . ."

"Until what?"

"Until you caught me and made our bargain."

"What is our bargain?"

"You released me. Now I'll help you undo your mother's magic and free you."

"How?"

"Simple. You bring me one single hair from your mother's head. With it I can grant your wishes. There are lots of things you want. Your mother has kept you tied hand and foot, because the spell she put on you exhausted her powers. She, who was a great enchantress, became not merely a mortal but a timid, frightened shadow of a mortal. Look how she's got you in that after-school care center. No friends because friends might 'get you into trouble.'" His voice rose in a cruel imitation of the worried tones in which Rob's mother usually spoke. "Or," he continued slyly, "friends might take you away from her. Just look at your life, boy!"

Rob nodded. Every day, for as long as he could remember, he had wished he could make his life different.

"With each wish you make and I grant, the enchantment holding you will grow weaker, until you are free, free to grow up, to have your own life, just what you've always wanted."

"What if I ask my mother to release me?" asked Rob.

"Alone, she can't. She's now a prisoner of her own spells. Believe me. Mine is the only way."

"And my father?"

"The enchantment still makes it impossible for anyone to mention that subject to you. Now bring me that single hair, and then sleep."

"Not so fast!" Rob balked. "How do I know you're telling the truth? You could still be a bad dream. How did you wish away that smelly stuff? You had power for that?"

"Good thinking!" grinned the creature. "I have a tiny bit of knowledge of magic of my own, enough to take the zotum away but not nearly enough to free you. I cannot, for example, simply take a hair of your mother's head. You must give it to me. As for the truth of what I say, listen. Your birthday is in three days, which is why I must rush you. If you are not free by your birthday, then once again you will grow one year younger. It will be as if this year of your life never existed. Your mother will move with you to another place, and begin life over, and after that year, move and begin over, and over, as each year you remain a child under her spell. With my help, you can break the enchantment. Believe me! Go look in the folder where your mother keeps your school papers. You'll see. She has already thrown this year's papers away. You'll find darned little past for yourself, none for her. You'll find no dates on photographs. And friends? Have you never wondered that your mother gets neither letters nor visits from old friends? Why not? Go, boy! Look! Look in the papers. How long do you think you have lived in this stuffy house? Forever? No. One year. You were allowed to grow from baby to big boy—of that you have memories—but you'll grow no farther. You'll never be free . . . Unless you let me help you. Now. Bring me the hair!"

Rob, reluctantly, went to the files. He'd been brought up not to pry. How could he touch his mother's things? But, he had to know! There was the file of school papers, neatly labelled—nothing from this year. From kindergarten one faded, brittle drawing, no date. And these few others, all undated. Photo album. No date. Nothing in the pictures gave time or place. He was always alone, in swimsuit or pajamas, a somber little boy, alone. Another file. Rent receipts for this house. One year. Rob put away the folders, walked barefoot across the freezing floor to his mother's room. He hesitated. His mother a powerful enchantress? From the pillow beside her head, Rob took one strand of hair, and returned with it to the creature, who bowed his thanks.

"Do you have a name?" Rob asked.

"Baa-vek."

"Goodnight, Baa-vek. And Baa-vek, you won't use my mother's hair to harm her, will you?"

"Harm? No. Only to free you. You'll see. With my help you will not be trapped on your birthday, but free. Sweet dreams, Rob."

Sweet dreams? Rob wanted to laugh.

Then Rob slept.

In the darkness Baa-vek held up the single strand of hair. His eyes glittered with joy. It had begun.

Rob slept. Rob who was docile and obedient, whose handsome face was so often clouded with worry. Rob was the boy who stood alone, his fists clenched at his sides, watching the rest of the world. Rob had never been dirty. It wasn't allowed. Rob had never even lost a mitten, but had simply worn, as unprotesting as a puppet, the security strings through his jackets. Every morning he went to school, then to the after-school program. Every evening he waited for his mother to pick him up in front of the school. He stood alone, listening to the mournful ping ping of the empty metal clips as the flag rope was blown against the flagpole.

Every night he and his mother drove home, to the closed-up smell of their cramped little house. Rob hung around outside as long as possible, claiming always that he was looking for just one more perfect horsechestnut burr to add to his collection, which filled a basket on the dining table. Rob stayed outside until his fearful mother called him in. He hoped she had the heat on or the oven going, anything to take away the cold, moldy smell that was home. Nothing ever did.

Every dinner was balanced and bland, straight from the freezer. Rob dreamed of soups and sauces simmering, and of fresh bread. Years ago, before he'd gone to school, Rob had stayed every day with a no-nonsense babysitter, who ordered him from morning till night. "No nonsense now, Robert. Pick up your feet!" Along with his mother, she had kept him from dirt, from climbing trees, from play with water, strings, ropes and sticks, and from making loud noises. Rob remembered the food at her house. It had been every bit as uninspired as his mother's cooking. So Rob had dreamed and waited. Until he met Baa-vek, Rob had been certain that soon his overprotective mother would realize that he was old enough. Finally she would let him take over the cooking. Ahhhhh . . . But now . . . forever a child? Forever? Rob shuddered in his sleep. Sleep.

Morning.

Rob overslept. The house was rain dark and cold. Silence. Rob jumped out of bed, pulled on his clothes, and ran to his mother's room. She was not awake, although her alarm clock buzzed incessantly.

"Mother! Mother! Wake up. It's late!"

Louder.

"Mother! Wake up! We're late."

Slowly, she stirred. Rob could not believe it. His mother was never late. She'd be upset. He ran to put the kettle on, to set the table, tucking in his shirt as he went.

"Ohh," his mother sighed. "How could I have slept so long? Thanks for doing breakfast, Rob." She kissed his cheek. "Such a big boy."

Rob stiffened. How did she mean that? "And nearly bigger," he added. "In three days I'll be . . ."

"Oh." His mother cut him off. "Yes. How time flies. In three days. We must do something special. Ready, Rob?"

With that she led the way out of the house and into the car. They rode in silence to the school. Rob spent the first hour slumped at his desk with his head in his hands, brooding.

"Rob?" It was Baa-vek, invisible, whispering in his ear. "How about a skateboard? Out in warm sunshine on a gentle hill? Something your mother never would let you do. I'll tell you just how to word the wish, and when you're finished—flick—back in school without being missed."

Rob wished.

It was splendid. He seemed made for the skateboard. Whirl, dip, glide, turn. There, how smoothly he went in a sunny, empty world. When he got tired and hungry, Rob found himself back in school. No one had missed him. He did notice that along with the skateboard, his sox had disappeared from his feet, but it seemed a small price to pay for such a morning.

Rob spent the remainder of the day thinking about Baa-vek and wishes still a bit off. He also thought about his mother. He had always loved her. How could she have done such a thing? A child forever? Not ever old enough to be alone in the house or to ride his bike the three short miles to town? He had to confront her. Tonight. Definitely.

As usual, none of the other kids seemed to have anything to say to him, and, as usual, he had no idea what he could say to them.

That evening Rob was first inside the house. He had wished away the closed, stale smell that had choked it. Rob carried his mother's briefcase to the living-room couch. Tonight, right after dinner he'd tell her he knew, demand to be free. Yes. Right after dinner.

"Your briefcase weighs a ton." He tried to sound the way he always did. How did he usually sound?

"Yes, it's filled with work I must finish by tomorrow." She sighed. Then, barely inside the room, she sank into a chair, sighing once again. "I must have spring fever. I'm so tired."

"I'll do dinner," suggested Rob.

"Thanks, dear." She didn't even seem surprised.

For an instant Rob was stunned. Yes! Maybe everything was okay after all. Maybe she didn't plan to keep him a baby. She'd just said yes. Rob ran for the refrigerator, opened it: one dead carrot, an equally dead scallion, two eggs, half a carton of milk. But maybe he could make a soup. A look into the cupboard showed not a single can of broth, nothing.

"It's getting late, Rob." insisted Baa-vek. "And you are

so hungry. For tonight why don't you just wish the dinner. After all every wish brings you that much closer to being free, and tomorrow . . ."

"Yes. Tomorrow," he agreed, "I'll wish myself out of the after-school program and home. I can cook the whole dinner myself, and have time to read, and . . ." he shrugged, "time just to mess around."

Baa-vek smiled his little goat smile. "Yes, indeed."

"Can you tell me about my father?" Rob asked. "I've always imagined he lives in a forest somewhere and will come to get me as soon as . . . I always wondered why he didn't come."

"We cannot speak of it yet." Baa-vek looked away into the distance. "Your mother's power is still too great."

The dinner Rob wished was delicious, except for the dessert, peach pie. Rob took one bite as he was cutting the pieces to serve. "Arghhh. It's so salty." Rob didn't have the heart to throw it away, so he wished it gone, thinking that anyway it might be difficult to explain to his mother how he'd had time to bake. She, however, had eaten the dinner quietly and excused herself to return to her work. Rob cleared the table and started to wash the dishes.

Baa-vek urged him to wish them clean, but Rob needed time to think. Just what would he say to his mother? Ask her? No, tell her he knew? Rob tried different beginnings until he found one that seemed right.

But, when Rob left the kitchen, he found his mother asleep over her work. He stood there looking at her, a stocky, little woman, tired and grey. Was she really the woman in the dreams, tall and hard, with a threatening beauty?

"Mother," he said. "You've fallen asleep. You should go to bed," he hesitated, then added "unless you want to talk?" There. He was trying to ask her, even if it wasn't exactly confronting her. She didn't seem to notice, but sighed.

"Yes. Yes. Sleep. Goodnight, dear." She kissed him as she dreamily made her way into her own room.

Rob looked around the living room, at his mother's work, unfinished, on the table.

"Movie?" Baa-vek's soft whisper came from behind Rob's left shoulder.

"Won't somebody see me and get me in trouble?" asked Rob.

"Nope. Look at the newspaper. Here's a good one."

"Shouldn't I do something about my mother's work? Or will the wish get the job messed up the way the pie was?" asked Rob. He wanted the movie, but felt guilty and uncomfortable.

"Look. Just wish for the work to be done. Then we'll go to the movie. You've been kept on such a short leash that you can't even enjoy freedom. Nothing will go wrong. My powers are strong enough that I won't make a slip."

Rob wished.

"See," said Baa-vek when they had returned home. "What did I tell you? No one noticed. Did you like the movie?"

"Yes, thank you."

"You don't sound very enthusiastic."

"Really. Thank you." Rob hesitated. Baa-vek's yellow eyes glittered as he waited. Rob continued. "Skateboarding and movies alone are a little sad. But thanks, really."

"My pleasure." Baa-vek bowed.

"If you'll excuse me," said Rob, "I'll go to sleep now."

"Of course." Baa-vek seemed to hesitate. "But, Rob, if we are to free you by the time your birthday arrives, I must ask you for one more thing."

Rob looked at the yellow eyes. "What's that?"

"That strand of your mother's hair, was it plucked from her head?"

"Plucked? No. That might have hurt her. I found it on the pillow. Won't it do?"

"Yes, I suppose it will have to do. May I ask for one of yours as well? One from your head if you don't mind?"

"Sure." Rob pulled out a hair and handed it to Baa-vek. "Why?"

"I'll use it to free you. The magic your mother wove about you is extraordinarily powerful. You are, yourself, fairly brimming with it."

"Then why can't I free myself?"

"You don't," said Baa-vek, as he disappeared from sight, "know how."

Rob sighed. "No, I don't. I don't know anything much."

Once more Rob went through his mother's files. He found nothing. With pencil and paper he returned to his room, sat down at his desk, and began a list called WHAT I KNOW. Know?

Even the word was suspect. Rob crossed it out and wrote a new heading: BAA-VEK: (1) Says I'm under a spell my mother made, that I'll be a child forever; (2) grants wishes, which sometimes go a bit wrong; (3) says my wishes weaken the enchantment; and (4) says he needs hair of my mother's head and one of mine to free me. Why? While writing the question mark, Rob fell asleep. Rob did not dream.

Morning.

Rob raised his head from his desk. His shoulders were stiff, his whole body damp, cold and uncomfortable.

Rain again.

Again it was late. Hurriedly he dressed, then ran to his mother's room. For the second time his mother had overslept. Try as he might, Rob could not waken her.

"Rob." It was Baa-vek's voice, reassuring. "Rob. Don't worry. Just wish and she'll be safe and sound at work."

"Nothing will go wrong? She won't be in funny clothes or missing something she needs?" asked Rob.

"Nothing. I'm prepared, completely prepared, for this wish."

It was so easy that way. Rob wished.

The house was still. His mother, her briefcase, and her car were gone.

"Again, Rob!" urged Baa-vek. "Wish again and it's school . . . unless . . . the skateboard again? or maybe sailing? A boy with your spirit will love sailing. Come on, Rob, just wish."

Rob wished.

Baa-vek was right. Rob loved sailing, and did not mind at all being alone. Waves. Sunlight. Wind, stronger as Rob grew more confident. Silky. The quick response of the little boat. When he'd had enough, Rob swam. Rob swam alone, the boy who'd never been permitted to do anything dangerous swam alone.

The after-school program didn't exist for Rob that day. He forgot the program, forgot his plan to go home to cook. Rob barely managed to make it back to the school to wait for his mother.

In the car his mother said nothing of his birthday. Rob, feeling high spirited after his day, dared to ask her, reminded her that she'd said they would do something special for his birthday. Seeming not to hear him, she made no reply.

Once they were at home, Rob silently followed her into the house. Dropping to the couch, she sighed, "I'll just rest a minute here," and fell asleep.

Rob stood there a moment looking at her, then went to

the kitchen. In the refrigerator were the same dead carrot and scallions, the same two eggs he had seen yesterday.

"For an omlette," he muttered, "I'll need . . ."

"Planning to cook?" Baa-vek appeared, a cheerful grin on his pointed face.

"Yes, and I forgot to come home early, but an omlette and salad would be fine."

"Indeed they would. Well, wish away, dear boy, wish away."

Rob didn't know why, but he didn't especially like Baa-vek's hearty cheerfulness. Nevertheless, Rob wished, and the groceries appeared. Rob cooked, set the table, and tried repeatedly to awaken his mother.

"Thanks dear . . . not hungry . . . lunch at the office . . ." she replied in fragments punctuated by yawns and sighs.

Baa-vek disappeared. Rob ate alone.

After dinner Rob managed to waken his mother enough to get her to bed. Her hands were unpleasantly cold, her face pale.

"Spring fever," she murmured.

Baa-vek reappeared, suggested bowling, but Rob declined. There were so many questions.

"Tomorrow?" he asked. "On my birthday. Will I get younger?"

"It has always happened on the night after your birthday, while you sleep. That sleep erases all memory. She moves you while you sleep."

"And how will it be this year, now that I know, and now that you . . ."

"Now that I am helping you, you will wake up here one year older, a powerful boy."

"And my mother?"

"She'll accept it. She won't be able to stop you any more.

Ahhhh," Baa-vek yawned. "You've had a big day, my boy. Time for some sleep."

With that, Baa-vek was gone.

Rob straightened the chairs in the living room, picked up the newspapers and put them on the back porch. Walking back into the kitchen, he filled a glass with water, drank it, rinsed the glass, dried it and put it away.

Rob walked slowly to his room. Tomorrow would be the birthday that would make him free. Why didn't things seem better? Tomorrow he had to talk to his mother, first thing in the morning. Restless, he returned to the living room, and fiddled with the basket of horsechestnuts on the dining table. First in a circle, then in rows, he lined them up. Usually he liked to read, but not tonight. He could call Baa-vek back to play chess. No. Then why not wish his mother would wake up. *Then* they could talk. No, but why not? Because I'm scared to face her.

Putting the prickly burrs back into the basket, Rob turned off the lights and went to bed. He could lie there in the dark and think. Maybe he could find the words to talk to his mother. It would be great if he could be excited and happy about his birthday.

Morning.

Rain.

Again, it was late. Still in his pajamas, Rob went to waken his mother.

He stood at the open door of her room. She lay without moving.

"Mother. It's morning," he called to her, walked over, shook her shoulder gently. "Come on. Time to get up. I really have to ask you something important. Please wake up."

Nothing Rob did could rouse her. He ran to the kitchen, made coffee, hoping the smell would awaken her. Perhaps it helped because finally, after repeated urging, she smiled, sniffed and opened her eyes. Overjoyed, Rob offered her the coffee. She stretched, smiled, yawned. And then she closed her eyes again. "No. Mother! Don't go back to sleep! It's late. Wake up."

No response.

Rob went back to the kitchen to make breakfast. The orange juice was frozen solid. Rob tried without success to pry the lid off the can. It did not budge. He used one tool after another. Nothing worked. Frustrated, he pried at the lid with a knife, which slipped. Rob cried out in surprise and pain as blood filled the wound. Rob sucked his finger. Each time he took it from his mouth, more blood flowed into the cut. Grabbing a paper napkin, Rob wrapped his finger, then finished making the orange juice. Of course the frozen lump refused to melt. The more he stirred it, the angrier Rob got. Abandoning the orange juice, he ran to check on his mother.

She was very still. Her face had a greenish tinge; her lips were grey.

"Mother!"

Rob found a mirror, held it over her lips. A faint mist appeared on the glass.

"You could wish her at work," Baa-vek whispered.

"A wish?" demanded Rob. The blood from his cut finger had soaked the paper napkin. Looking around for a handkerchief, for something to use as a bandage, Rob shouted, "Right now I wish I'd never even started to make that blasted orange juice!"

At once Rob's finger was clean. There was no cut, no blood, no blood-soaked napkin.

Baa-vek smiled his little goat smile. "See? All done. Now, shall we get this big day started?"

"No. Things are worse since I've been wishing. My

mother's sick. Look at her. She's pale as death, Baa-vek. She's been weaker and weaker since you came. Have you made her sick? and . . . Baa-vek?"

"Rob."

"You said your power grew."

"Yes."

"It grows because you're taking the magic my mother put around me?"

"Yes."

"But your power also comes from her, from my mother, because she's getting weaker. Baa-vek, is she dying?"

"Certainly not. You still are not free Rob. It was a monstrous, powerful magic. She did a terrible thing to you Rob."

"But that power, the power that binds me. Does she have to die to end it?"

"Rob . . ."

"Does she?"

"You," he whispered. "Can't you feel the power all around you? Use it Rob! You can have a wonderful life!"

"Is SHE dying!?"

Baa-vek nodded his shaggy head.

"You. You aren't doing this to help me. You take the power from her for yourself. Right? You must kill her for YOUR power. I don't need to kill her to be free! That can't be the way it works! I won't kill her and I won't stay a child forever!"

Rob picked up his mother's limp hands, put his face close to hers. "Mother. I wish . . . I wish myself in your place! I give back all the wishes! Baa-vek! Give my mother her life!"

As he fell Rob smelled that closed-up musty smell their house had always had, heard Baavek's voice grow faint, "Nooooooooooo."

*   *   *

When Rob opened his eyes, he found himself on the dining-room floor, his head against the leg of the overturned dining-room table. His left hand, which was clenched under his back, burned like fire. Slowly Rob sat up, brought his hand to where he could examine it. From inside his fist came a small, insistent voice, "Rob. Rob. It mustn't end like this. We can do so much, so much. You'll be sorry. She has won. You'll be a baby, a baby forever!"

"No I won't. I won't give up," Rob insisted.

With his right hand, Rob fumbled for one of the horsechestnut burrs that lay scattered on the floor. At his touch, it opened. Carefully, Rob brought his hands together and closed the burr over the hot mass in his left hand. Shakily, Rob stood up. Holding the burr carefully, he walked into his mother's room. She lay as she had been, but breathed now as one does in a healthy sleep. Her lips were no longer grey.

"Baa-vek," said Rob. "I can think of only one thing to do with you."

With that he carried the horsechestnut burr to the back porch and took a large shovel from its place on the wall. Barefoot, sinking ankle deep into the mud, and enjoying every step of it, Rob took the burr far behind the house. He walked deep into the woodsy swamp where lake, canal, and river meet. In an open place he dug a hole quite deep and put the horsechestnut into it.

"Now, Baa-vek. Here you can grow, grow smaller. A tiny bit of you will go into every seed for as long as the tree lives."

With that Rob filled the hole with mud and rotting leaves. When he was done, he scraped his shovel against a tuft of long, coarse grass to clean the mud from it. Then, with the shovel on his shoulder, he returned to the house to care for his mother and to wait for the night of his birthday.

Within seven days, a towering horsechestnut tree grew in that clearing. It bloomed pale-pink clusters of blossom, like so many elaborate candelabra, then sent forth horsechestnut burrs, each finer than the other. The burrs rolled and tumbled far from the woodsy swamp. In each of them there was a voice, faint, but still calling.

IN HER BELFRY

*W*hen, exactly, is someone "generous to a fault," and did Bernice McCrudden qualify? And the whole question of punishment: Is generosity really a fault to be punished?

True, Bernice was unfailingly generous. When her children asked to "have a friend over," Bernice McCrudden replied, "Sure! Sure, they can come. They can all come! They can come for dinner, spend the night; they can move in!"

It was, therefore, more or less in the normal course of life that Bernice McCrudden found herself the sole adult one summer in the little log cabin she and her husband had built high in the Adirondack Mountains on a narrow, silver lake. Her husband had been called away to Japan on business, leaving Bernice in the cabin with her own children, her niece and nephew, and her children's friends.

The days passed pleasantly enough, and the evenings, too, though Bernice might have admitted to herself that she found them a bit long. Indeed, she yearned for those quiet hours to herself after the children were asleep.

All too often it was eleven o'clock at night before Bernice had finished the campfire, the ghost stories, the marshmallows, heard the last of the giggles, and given the last drinks of water. It was eleven at night before all was finished and the cabin was quiet.

Bernice McCrudden sat down and sighed. Now came her time to be alone, to read and to think and perhaps to write letters, her own quiet time.

Outside, the night was thick, muggy, moonless, starless, with heat lightning beyond the rim of distant peaks. Outside, the mosquitos hummed against the screen in great grey clouds, each mosquito driven to find her meal of blood so that she could lay her thousands of eggs. Inside, Bernice sat under the gas light, reading.

Whrrrrrr, Whrrrrr

Bernice looked up.

There was a bat in the cabin.

It seemed to be confused by the light. The poor creature flew back and forth, round and round, never seeming able to find the way it had come in.

"Oh, no," groaned Bernice. "Why now? Why tonight? I don't want to go to bed."

But who can sit under the gaslight reading while a frightened bat flutters to and fro above one's head?

Bernice knew all about a bat in the cabin. There was just one way to get it out: Bernice had to turn off the gaslight, open the doors, and, in the darkness, to wait.

Bernice knew that if one quietly and calmly does those things, after a time the bat will find its bearings and fly out into the night to find its food.

Whrrrrr, Whrrrrr

Bernice turned off the gaslight. Bernice opened the screen doors, propped each one open with a large piece of firewood, and stood outside, waiting.

Mosquitos, drawn by the scent of a cabin full of fine, young, warm blood, rushed inside, except for the swarm that enveloped Bernice.

Whrrrrr, Whrrrrr

Poor little bat. Something seemed to confuse it. Time

and again it fluttered up to one or another of the six windows that looked over the lake.

Poor Bernice, devoured by mosquitos, waited by the open door. It was too dark, too muggy, too heavy with mosquitos to go canoeing. Besides, what if one of the guest children woke up frightened, and did not find her in the cabin? She could take a quick swim, but she didn't want to swim. She wanted to sit down in the cabin and have her own time reading under the gaslight.

Whrrrrrr Whrrrr

The bat remained inside.

Defeated, Bernice returned to the dark cabin, leaving both doors open. Carefully, she unrolled her sleeping bag on the couch near the door. Even though Bernice knew that bats don't fly into one's hair, she found herself crouching low while the bat flew around and above her, never making it out the doors.

Bernice sat on the edge of her bed in the dark, waiting.

Whrrrr Whrrrr

Beer makes you sleepy, thought Bernice after an hour of sitting in the dark. Bent low, Bernice crept over to the refrigerator and opened the door. Taking out a beer, she closed the refrigerator and backed over to her sleeping bag. There she sat, on her bed in the dark, sipping the beer while the bat and the mosquitos feasted in the cabin.

"You don't need to eat on your way," whispered Bernice to the bat. "There are lots of mosquitos left outside."

Whrrrrrrrrrrrrr

Feeling she had no other choice, Bernice McCrudden lay down to sleep. It was a bad sleep, made unpleasant by the hot, muggy night air and by the mosquitos that fed upon her even though Bernice had covered her head with the sheet that lined her sleeping bag. The sheet made her hot but it did not keep out the buzz of the mosquitos.

"Little bat. It is partially because of you that I am hiding under this sheet," she had said as she covered her head. "Little bat I just know you don't have rabies, and yet . . . please don't drop your saliva, or anything else, on me tonight. Just fly out."

With that, Bernice slept.

Abruptly, Bernice was awake and listening, absolutely rigid with the intensity of her listening.

Whrrrr Whrrr

Whrrrr Whrrrr

Two pair of wings, two bats in the cabin. Two bats feeding on mosquitos.

"No!" said Bernice, sitting up. "No. Go outside, both of you! Out! . . . . please."

Whrrr Whrrr

Whrrr Whrrr

And Bernice, who had always said welcome to every child, to every stray animal, to everyone, lay back down and covered her head. Then, throwing off the covers, Bernice sat up on the couch. Hadn't she just read about it? About the house someone had bought just over the mountain. The neighbors had come, the newspaper wrote, come to welcome the new owners. After the hellos, the newspaper reported, the first thing the neighbors said to the new owners was, "What're you gonna do about the bats?"

The new owners had rushed to count the bats coming out of their attic that night, and had stopped counting at one thousand. The newspaper reported that the new owners had called a bat expert to come help them send the bats away, but before the expert arrived the bats had left.

Bernice lay back down on her sleeping bag and listened.

Whrrr Whrrr

Whrrr Whrrr

Whrrr Whrrr

Bernice McCrudden listened to three sets of wings. "No!" cried Bernice. She stood up and shook her sheet at the bats. "No!"

Whrrr Whrrr/Whrrr Whrrr
Whrrr Whrrr/Whrrr Whrrr

In the doorway two more little bats fluttered a moment before entering the cabin.

Bernice retreated under the covers.

Throughout the night she listened and counted. Just before dawn Bernice, who was generous to a fault, said aloud, as forcefully as she could, "Now look fellows. See! See the outside! Now can you find your way out?"

But Bernice McCrudden, who knew something about bats, knew that at dawn bats do not go outside. No, indeed, at dawn bats go inside. They go high, high into the rafters where they fold up like tiny little leaves to sleep away the day until night when they once again fly in search of food.

Whrrrrrrrrrrrrr

OVERTURE

❧

prised, ever so slightly wrinkled her nose. She had no doubt noticed a peculiar smell, which permeated my clothing and beard after my long association with those chickens.

Releasing my grasp, I hailed a passing car, hurled the crate of squawking chickens into the back seat, and jumped into the front seat beside the driver. "Quick, man!" I shouted at him. "Drive me to the medical center. I'm an old man and injured!" I was not injured, of course, but needed to leave quickly and to rid myself of the chickens.

The astonished driver clashed the gears of his car in his rush to obey.

"Thank you, dear lady!" I cried once more from the open car window.

I had felt so awkward, so embarrassed before that elegant lady, whose whole life, all her dreams and thoughts, had come from her heart and mind to mine when I seized her hands. What I had learned of her and of her husband, Maestro Henry Grimelda, was more wonderful that anything I'd ever dreamed. They were musicians, earth-world famous, with everything anyone could want. Except. Except they had once dreamed of having a child, a child who'd be musical, of course, but no child had come. Now they believed themselves to be too old. Nothing could be more perfect, nothing in the wide universe!

Having left Madame to go about her business, I set to work, and then to watch, and to hope for my own dream.

It was quite early the next morning when a pajama–clad little boy appeared beside the bed in which Madame and Maestro Grimelda slept.

"Mommy, Poppi. Could we wake up now? I'm hungry."

Both Madame and Henry sat straight up in bed. First they looked at the boy, who was small, somewhat mischievous about the eyes, with a mop of brown hair that was definitely shaggy. Then they looked at each other.

Madame shook her head. "No. I did not . . ."

"How did you get here, little boy?" asked Henry in a voice gruff from sleep.

"I am yours."

"But how? Surely you have a mother."

"I'm not sure how. Uncle Crumple made me out of something. I'm not sure what. He said you needed a boy, and that he had never made one before, but that I seemed a pretty good job."

"Henry!" cried Madame in alarm. "We'll be imprisoned for kidnapping. We could not even repeat such a story. Ohhhh!"

"Calm yourself, my dear," soothed Maestro.

I was delighted to hear him. Clearly Maestro Henry Grimelda was a man who accepted the power of magic and then proceeded to order his life accordingly. He and I would get along splendidly.

"Could we have breakfast while you decide if you want me?" asked the boy, one large brown eye visible through the tangle of his hair.

"Breakfast, of course!" replied Henry. "Waffles?"

"Pancakes?" replied the boy. "They're easier."

"Pancakes it is," said Henry, putting on his robe. "Do you have a name?"

"I like Jeff. I'd like to be Jeff, if you don't mind."

"Your mother," said Henry, "taught you very good manners, Jeff."

"No, I have no other mother. Uncle Crumple said you'd want a child with good manners so he had to make one. It took all yesterday afternoon. He was in a lather!" The boy laughed. I was embarrassed. He needn't have told that.

By the time Madame appeared in the kitchen, breakfast

was ready, the table set. She sat, not saying a word, looking at the boy over the rim of her teacup. She could not look at her husband because it would hurt him to see in her eyes how much she wanted to keep the little boy, Jeff.

Jeff, meanwhile, piled stack after stack of pancakes on his plate, sloshed them with maple syrup, and ate them, pausing now and then to praise them.

"Uncle Crumple said you'd be the kind of father who'd make me a pancake that spells my name, and you did. It's delicious."

After breakfast was cleared away, Jeff walked over to Madame Grimelda. To her astonishment and delight, he was suddenly up on a kitchen stool giving her a great hug.

"Are you sorry? Do you wish I'd go away?" he asked her.

Maestro Grimelda, who knew of his wife's excesses, tried to stop her. Dropping the spatula he was drying, he rushed across the kitchen to reassure them both. He was too late.

Madame Grimelda hugged Jeff, and, with her voice full of tears, whispered, "Go away? Oh, no. I adore you. I wish I had eight more just like you!"

Prepared for just such an expression of family love, and full of my wonderful plan, I hastened to fulfill her wish.

With an earth-shattering crash, I made that dining room alive with eight more little boys, all jumping and yelling, all naked as jaybirds. I had not mastered delivering humans fully clothed. Jeff let out a whoop. "More boys. Brothers!" Madame Grimelda turned pale.

"I always knew that someday you'd exaggerate once too often," muttered her husband.

"Oh, Henry," Madame cried, "they'll cost a fortune just in sneakers!"

Another crash, and the dining room floor was littered

with shoes and clothes of all colors, most of it shabby enough to please any boy. With much scuffling, the boys dressed themselves.

"I don't believe it," declared Madame. "We are hallucinating. There was some mysterious and possibly fatal bacteria in my ryebread flour, no doubt."

She looked in amazement at her husband. He was smiling.

"Hmmmm." His smile grew broader. "Wonder if they are musical?"

"Henry. You can't!"

Before she could say what he could not, I put in each boy's hand a musical instrument. Ah. A slight mistake. I could see it by the expression on Maestro's face.

"Four tubas, four cornets, and a viola?" he objected. Never! Not even Vivaldi could write for those!"

With that, I caused the instruments to disappear and gave others, one by one, to each boy as Maestro Grimelda nodded in approval or frowned in disbelief. When I, still invisible to all of them, had given each boy an instrument that satisfied the Maestro, I breathed a sigh of relief. I was learning about earthly music. The boys stood proudly.

"Now then," Henry commanded, "come with me."

Single file, the boys, bearing their instruments, followed him into the music room, with its two grand pianos and sliding doors to divide the room when two pianists needed privacy for practice. On the walls and side tables were antique instruments. The boys gazed in awe. Madame, looking somewhat dazed, lingered in the doorway.

"Come, come. Step forward, one by one. Tell us your name, and let us hear you play."

"Matt," said a large boy wearing thick glasses held in place by an elastic band around the back of his head. Although he moved a bit awkwardly, he held the oboe nicely and played smoothly and with real feeling. Maestro Grimelda nodded in approval.

"Anthony," said a fair boy, also tall and exceedingly thin, as he stepped forward with his bass viol. At the end of his piece, he looked at the floor. Madame's eyes glistened. Again Maestro Grimelda nodded his approval.

A third boy, with a dreamy expression and dreadful posture took half a step forward. "Nicholas," he whispered. He played the violin well, but a bit sloppily, as if only half trying.

Madame watched as her husband walked over to the boy, and made a small but important correction in the boy's position. The playing improved.

Maestro Grimelda nodded. The boy slumped back.

"Pete," grinned the next boy. He was short and muscular, his eyes and hair black. The face, Madame thought, came from Asia or perhaps Latin America. His playing of the French horn was fine, just fine. Madame began to smile. These boys were good.

Jeff sat on a piano bench, a cello between his knees. With a flourish, he began, hair flopping in his eyes as he bent over in concentration.

"Red," said the next boy, and he was. Framing his grinning, coffee-colored face, stiff, fire-colored hair stood up and out all over his head. His violin, too, was full of fire, sweet and hot. Madame stole a look at her husband.

"It's a dream, but he is enjoying it," she muttered, afraid to let herself believe for moment what she heard and saw.

"Ken," said the next boy, with the clarinet already at his lips.

Madame sighed ecstatically. "Another. How well we dream."

"Alfred," said the last boy, as he stepped forward. His flute made the group complete.

"Now, Mama, while you look for some appropriate music for us, I shall take the boys for a walk before lunch. How about it boys? To the swinging bridge?"

Before Madame could mention the lack of boots and jackets, I caused to appear on the floor of the front hall a mass of scuffed boots and thick jackets mixed together with hats and gloves. The boys scrambled, and swapped, laughing, until there remained a solitary, too small and very torn mitten, which I quickly made disappear.

Jacketed and booted, the boys trooped outside, each of them giving to Madame a hug and a kiss as he passed. When Maestro embraced her, she whispered, "It can't be a dream. They all smell like boys." He kissed her once again and followed the boys, closing the door behind him. Madame stood there alone in the quiet of the front hall.

Making myself visible, I bowed rather awkwardly because of the bottle, and said to her, "They are real. I know. I made them."

It was an old-fashioned bottle of bluing with the cork shoved well down the neck, and I intended to put it somewhere safe. "They are real," I repeated, "and a pretty good job, too."

"You?" She was astonished to see me. "Where are your chickens?"

"Ornamental fowl," I corrected. "I left them in the car with the man I commanded to drive me."

"Why?"

"I was free of them, of the curse."

"What curse?"

"You did see me with those chickens!" I replied. "That was the curse. We're old adversaries, Tremor and I, but that was his worst and most successful trick so far. Never mind. You were the only person in eons to be both kind enough and smart enough to help me, and to have something the chickens would eat. After I left you, I snagged Tremor, who used to lurk about to laugh at me with the chickens. Now I've trapped him, using the old earth-trick to get the genie in the bottle."

I held up the bottle for her inspection.

"I can only see bluing," she whispered.

"Good." I was pleased. "He's probably ashamed to be blue. Serves him right. I'll put him safely away. But, dear Madame, Tremor is not the reason I have come. I have, as you have seen, quite powerful magic of my own. I can be of tremendous help to you with your nine boys and this big house to run. I have such a longing to be part of a family. May I stay here and serve you?"

"You? You are very kind . . . ah . . ."

"Uncle Crumple, at your service." I bowed again.

"Uncle Crumple. Yes. We can use your help, but . . . ah . . . please . . ." She blushed, looking for the right words. I tried to help her.

"I understand," I replied. "You'd rather I did not read your mind and use my magic to grant thoughts or thoughtless 'wishes' but just to help out in an earthly way, more or less?"

"Yes," sighed Madame, obviously relieved, "Yes. That's it exactly."

"You won't mind," I asked, "if I use my magic powers to do the housekeeping?"

"Not in the least." Madame sighed.

There. I'd done it, given them not just one musical child, but nine. In fact I had created a large, wonderful family, and now I could live with them and be with them. In that crate I'd seen it all. The chickens and I had seen it all. The crate, which had been hammered together out of chicken wire, boards, and whatnot, had contained one solid piece of fine wood from an earthly television set. As is the way with such waves and particles, things had clung to that wood, and thus the ornamental fowl and I had seen hundreds of hours of family television comedies. We loved them. I longed to be in such a family.

Ah, but first I had to put Tremor where he could not escape. The cellar seemed the ideal spot. I took Tremor, trapped in the bluing bottle, down the stairs into the darkest corner of the cellar, where no one would ever find him.

After that little chore, I joined Madame. We went upstairs, where we used her good sense and my magic powers to create bedrooms and a fine library-study for the boys, and a comfortable room for me.

By the time Maestro and the boys returned from the forest, Madame had sheet music ready for their first practice together. I made myself invisible to listen, and reappeared in time to have dinner ready for the table.

Of the boys, Jeff knew me the best, as he'd taken me the longest time to complete. But all of them were glad to see me and greeted my dinner with enthusiasm. The boys ate tremendous amounts. I looked around at them with inexpressible joy.

Now I was free of Tremor's curse and had safely imprisoned him. What's more, I was in full command of my own magic powers and intended to participate in earthly joys. Here was a family. I'd be in the kitchen, in the center, helpful, wise, and funny just like all those television families I'd seen. Madame and Maestro would continue as concert pianists; the boys would grow; and I'd be right there in the middle of an earthly family.

For many years, it seemed I had succeeded. The boys went to school. Madame and Maestro spent the better part of their days pretty much as they had, practicing the piano and taking care of the business end of being concert artists.

Using my magic powers, I was housekeeper, gardener,

and did most of the cooking. Madame supervised the boys' homework, claiming I was too soft a touch for the job. She said all the boys needed to do was to look at me with sad eyes and I would use my magic power to do their school work or homework for them. Poof, she said, and the homework was done. She exaggerated, of course. I was discreet with my help.

Maestro was their music teacher. After dinner, they made music, the whole family together. For me, those evenings were bliss. When the family came home from school or travels, I was in the center of the family. Sometimes I told the boys stories of my previous existence and of my conflicts with Tremor, but never where he was. Often they asked if I missed my old opponent. "Not once," I replied, and it was true.

To keep the boys healthy, there was good food, long walks, sports, and a spoonful of my special tonic after breakfast. When Nick protested that I had the power to make it taste good, I was offended. How could the boy not know that those tonics only work if they taste vile?

The boys were different one from another in size and in temperament, and the music heard in that house ranged from Bach to Alfred's compositions, which included a memorable Rock-a-Bach Baby. Did I ever feel nostalgic for those old television comedy families? Did I ever watch summer reruns? Once. The minute the show began, I was overcome by the smell of musty chicken feathers, as if the fowl and I were once again shut up in that wretched crate. I turned off the set and never tried again.

Just when I was feeling the most confident, the most satisfied with my earthly life, smack in the center of a real family, it hit. Ah, yes, I *was* in the kitchen after school while the boys were having their snack. But I was not wise and funny; when I was not being violently shaken by sneeze after sneeze, I was, with red and itching eyes, collapsed against a kitchen cabinet. The boys were helping themselves to peanut butter from the jar and crackers from some box. A puddle of spilled milk, juice, or water stood next to every one of their glasses. The boys were sympathetic, but their natural high spirits made me weary. Suddenly a trumpet sounded. The boys sprinted toward the sound, which came from the front of the house. After a few minutes they returned, chagrined. "It was Mama," they reported. "She couldn't get in the front door because there was a lot of stuff in the way." No sooner were they back in the kitchen than Maestro appeared at the kitchen door. "Boys. I cannot drive into the garage. Please put away the tools and the projects, immediately. And don't block the garage next time." Again the boys sprinted.

I sneezed uncontrollably.

When Madame and Maestro came into the kitchen a moment later, I was still leaning against the cabinet, weak from sneezing, my eyes streaming.

"Sorry for all the mess," I apologized.

"The boys' messes are not your responsibility, Uncle Crumple," replied Maestro. "Magic or no magic."

"Are you sick?" asked Madame.

A number of particularly violent sneezes prevented my answering. Once they had stopped, I, in complete despair wailed, "I can't cope, can't. What can we doooo?"

Madame spoke in her most soothing voice. "Come. We'll have a cup of tea. I have one especially for hay fever, which seems to be your problem."

All of us followed her. There, in the cool of the living room, everyone sat down with tea. The boys brought cold cloths for my itching eyes. Madame poured. After three cups, I was able to stop sneezing long enough to speak.

"Suddenly I have terrible sneezes and my eyes itch all the time. I cannot concentrate. I have lost my memory, my magic powers, and my sense of humor."

I was interrupted by another violent sneeze. "I could do everything, keep things tidy, cook, everything, as long as I had my powers. I don't know if the hay fever has weakened me or if I have been too long on your planet. Now I'm helpless! Do you see what that means?"

"There is no reason," repeated Maestro, "for you to clean up messes made by boys."

"But, the cooking, the garden, the laundry!" I protested.

"No problem," grinned Nick. He went into the laundry room, took the clean clothes out of the dryer and dumped them onto the breakfast-room table. Right, left, and center, nine boys took out socks, shirts, and towels, and folded them. Up they tromped to their rooms. "Done!" They returned.

"In nice weather we can hang them outside, and in foul weather we'll use the dryer. We can have teams for the washing, too," Nick said.

"See there, Uncle Crumple," crooned Madame. "We've let you do far too much. It's time you learned to supervise."

I sipped more tea, sniffled, blew my nose, and heaved one or two great sighs. "I'm finished," I said, "magically speaking!"

"No matter," Madame smiled. "If you want to stay with us, we'll make do. For now, see if you can sleep. A nap will certainly help. I'll cook dinner."

And so it was that I abandoned all attempts to use magic power. The hay fever continued, diminished only slightly by Madame's special teas or any other treatment we attempted. I tried to regain my sense of humor, and to be happily in the center of the family, wise and helpful. Some days I was more successful than others.

The boys did the laundry, some cleaning, and some gardening. I did most of the shopping, but the hay fever made me terribly forgetful. We often ran out of important things, so that someone was always rumaging in the second pantry in the cellar. Someone was always shouting that this or that should be added to the running grocery list we kept in the kitchen. Everyone added to it or directed someone else to add to it, and I took it with me shopping.

No one noticed, certainly I did not notice, when someone shouted "last of the bluing for the laundry! Add it to the list!" When I did shop, I did not wonder who had used bluing and where on earth he'd found it. I did not think of Wizard Tremor.

In the weeks that followed, I should have questioned many small mysteries. The television set was turned on at the oddest times of day and night. No one knew by whom.

Then, small, nasty things began to happen. Chores the boys had done were undone. Jeff knew he'd put the laundry away, but there it lay, back in a jumble on the table. Matt had cut the grass, and did a good job. Nick saw him do it. But when Maestro walked outside, he saw a ragged mess, which looked as if someone had cut the grass badly on purpose. Maestro scolded Anthony, who happened to be the first boy he saw after he saw the lawn. Anthony tried to find Matt to make him do it over. Failing to find Matt, Anthony had to cut the grass. Maestro saw him do a good job, but not an hour later Madame looked out at the ragged lawn and demanded to know why the grass had not been cut. Problems, problems, problems, and I had no magic to solve them.

"Who's been messing with my bow? It's unstrung!"

"I didn't! But somebody broke my E string and took my extra!"

"My reeds! They're ruined. After I worked for hours on

them. Okay, okay. Fine. Fine! No reeds, no oboe, and all of you can just eat worms!"

"My mouthpiece was in my case. Now who schnibbed it?"

"He did!"

"I didn't!"

No matter who was assigned to take care of the sheet music, the family was always one short when it came time to play together. Several times we found paper airplanes made from sheet music in the garden. All the boys denied doing it.

Worst of all was the hot water. You could check the boiler: full, water hot. You could go directly upstairs to the shower, and no sooner were you soapy than the hot water ran out.

And then, no matter what the game—cards, chess, checkers, Ping-Pong, billiards, or basketball—Red won. Red won even when he tried to lose. Somehow, somehow.

In those few weeks, nobody's mood was particularly cheerful, but all at once Matty outdid us all. Matty was sullen. Matty was mean. He was brutally cold to Madame and Maestro, ignored me, and fought continuously with his brothers. Now, if Matty had been merely mean, we might never have learned the truth, might have suffered much worse fates; but fortunately for all of us Matty also got lazy.

It was the last weekend of summer. On Saturday afternoon, the Grimeldas, all eleven of them, were to perform in a small auditorium on the university campus. For Sunday evening we'd planned to have a picnic feast in our garden. Things began well enough with the performance on Saturday. The audience listened with obvious pleasure, and demanded several encores. Clearly the musicians deserved a treat, so we went directly from the concert to the ice-cream parlor. Afterward, we returned home to the dark, silent house.

Upon opening the front door, we encountered a most dreadful, but to me most familiar, smell, and set off a horror of cackling and flapping. Chickens. The house was full of them, from rafters to tabletops, and more.

It took hours to get them out, hours more to clean up the disgusting mess. Of course I suspected Matty, but how could he have done it? He was with us, played well in fact. Actually he had been in a rare, cheerful mood. I watched for him during the clean-up. His portion was clean; he had done it awfully well and awfully fast. But still.

It was after midnight when the house seemed clean and we could sleep. On Sunday, while everyone prepared the food and tables for our picnic, I had planned to be of general help and to keep an eye on Matty, but was kept busy the whole day cleaning up the chicken droppings and feathers we had apparently missed. Finally the house was clean again, and I was clean. I went out to the garden.

It looked beautiful, with a feast set out on long tables under the trees: Madame's famous potato salad; Maestro's liver pâté; fried chicken à la Pete and Anthony; green salad from Alfred's own garden; corn on the cob that was husked, steamed, and hauled to the table by Nicholas; hundreds of strawberries that had been hulled, sugared, and lemoned by Jeff and Ken; and platters of sliced tomatoes with basil and dribbles of oil and vinegar, courtesy of Red. Candles in paper lanterns, the long white table cloths, the flowers of late summer. It was a picture to remember.

Then, in spite of an attack of sneezing and spluttering, I noticed Matty leaning against the Swamp Maple, sulking. "Matty!" I demanded. "Where's the lemonade? That's your specialty. I'd have expected you to have a most muscular arm today, after squeezing enough lemons to make lemonade for this crowd!"

Matty ignored me for a long minute and then slowly raised his eyes.

I waited. I stared him down in spite of two big sneezes. Matty went all red and hot on the back of his neck, but did not look away. I continued my stare, right into that boy's mind.

I know. I know. I'd promised Madame not to read their minds, and I'd kept that promise even when my magic powers were at their peak. Still, the hatred in Matty's eyes made me forget the promise, and forget that my magic was, I believed, gone. I looked, and what I saw gave me quite a start.

Matty was speculating: Should he use his magic first to turn me into a wart, or to wish for the lemonade to be too sweet to annoy his mama or too tart to annoy his brothers?

Helpless, I watched. Matty shrugged, turned his back on me.

Then, Matty wished, and jugs appeared, three on each of the long tables. Each jug, its sides dripping in the warm afternoon, was filled to the rim with lemonade, ice, and bright yellow slices of lemon.

And then Matty turned to face me. He looked long and hard at me with a face that said, "I dare you! Just ask me how I did that and you'll be a wart, a simple wart!"

I gazed in wonder at that boy, and all too slowly began to do some thinking of my own. He, Matty, had magic powers. But how? On his own? Maybe. But, the chickens? Matty's long, bad mood? It reminded me of someone else, *of Tremor.*

Leaving Matty glaring at everyone in sight, I beat it down the cellar stairs. It took less than a minute to see: in the basement trash, which of course everyone had forgotten to empty, was an old, empty bluing bottle. A new bottle stood on the shelf. No sign of Tremor. I ran back up the stairs.

Madame Grimelda turned, saw Matty, and smiled at him. She reached out to touch him. Matty pulled away. "Matty," she whispered, "please, tell me what's troubling you."

Matty shouted so that everyone turned to look. "You hate me! And I hate you! I hate all of you! And I wish you were . . . No I wish I was . . ."

"Matty!" I roared at him from the top of the cellar stairs. At top speed I sneezed my way across the lawn, and hurled myself up at him. Before Matty could say what he wished, I'd covered his mouth.

Finally, when he stopped struggling, I let Matty go. He fell heavily to the ground and buried his head in his arm. Madame sat down on the grass beside him and gently touched his shoulder. This time Matty didn't pull away.

I concentrated my energies upon finding Tremor. He couldn't be too far away, not the way he loved to watch whatever trouble he'd create.

As I searched for him, out of old habit I began to chant the ancient incantations and to realize that my own magic powers had been restored to me. I could think, could make myself invisible, and match my wits once more against Tremor.

It took considerable effort, especially because I could not completely stop my sneezing, but, after an enormous struggle I got Tremor by the nose and I knew what had to be done.

The next morning at breakfast I requested a family meeting for that evening, then returned to my room to complete my tasks. Matty came by to say he was sorry. Tremor had tricked him with dreams that seemed real. Those dreams convinced Matty that we were all his enemies. Tremor enabled Matty to use magic to play tricks on us. As Matty related them, Tremor's plans for the future were frightful, but he had drawn out his game because he believed me to be helpless.

After Matty left, Nick came in to say he was sorry. He'd been the one to use the bluing on the laundry, pulling out the cork that kept Tremor inside, but had neither seen nor heard Tremor make his escape.

After Nick left, I returned to my work. Time was short.

That night, we met in the music room, with its two grand pianos, the sliding doors to divide the room in half when two pianists wished to play separately, and the collection of antique musical instruments hanging on the walls.

I stood before them, feeling wretched that it was for the last time.

"Wizard Tremor is here," I began. "I've made sure he cannot show himself, nor speak, nor make magic, at least for the time we need. At this moment, my powers exist in full strength, enough to do what must be done. I have loved being part of an earthly family, but your world is no place for me. It gives me hay fever, and my magic powers disappeared and then returned without warning and according to no pattern I can understand. Never knowing just how much magic a fellow has is too disconcerting at my age. As for Tremor, he MUST go."

Everyone nodded somberly.

"I have thought how to send him . . . and . . ."

Suddenly my eyes were wet, but not from hay fever. Everyone waited while I refused Madame's large lace handkerchief, and wiped my eyes instead on the hem of my shirt.

"There is at midnight," I continued, "a hairline crack in

time. With my magic powers, and with musical power provided by all of you, I can push old Tremor through—if I go along. Here's what I've written to do the job." I handed out the sheets. All of them studied my first musical composition. I could tell they were speechless with admiration. "Pretty good, eh?" I had to clear my throat. "I'll miss you, all of you."

Then I had to blow my nose. The boys crowded around; we shook hands. I bowed to Madame, shook hands with Maestro. Madàme leaned forward, kissed me on both cheeks. "Thank you, thank you for everything," she said.

I blushed, had to blow my dratted nose again. Then, without further fuss, I continued.

"Here is what you'll need to blow us away. See. It is fortissimo, staccato, then fugues to keep us going, and see this sustained finale . . ."

The boys picked up the instruments I'd assigned.

Madame stood up with her sheet of music, and started to take it to the piano.

I looked at her one last time, that wonderful woman, and said, "Madame, dear Maestro. My love for earthly family life is undiminished . . ."

I made myself invisible, and felt Tremor struggling.

The notes were struck, the piece begun. I pushed Tremor ahead.

"It will be so lonely," I choked, "out there with Tremor . . . If only I could return . . . we could raise such . . ."

Up, up! in the rush of beautiful notes. "Aaachoooo!"

AND A NIGHTMARE

*T*here is, in a certain country, a chain of stores across the land. In cities and towns you can see them, and in the massive shopping centers of the big suburbs. You will find them among the run-down, ill-matched buildings on roads lined with gas stations, used-car lots, the occasional small house not yet become a business, and here and there the bleak remains of a farm. In some places the Needles, for that is the name of each of the stores in the chain, in some places the Needles is open all day and all night, and you may, if you wish, push your shopping cart up and down in wide, neon-lit aisles at four o'clock in the morning.

Whether the Needles is in a busy area where the store is open all day and all night, or in a quieter spot, where the doors close and the lights are put out when nighttime comes, wherever they are, the Needles store has a sign, tall and red, that stays lit, unblinking, by night and by day.

Here I am, a taxi driver in a certain country, driving five dazzlingly beautiful girls to a party. Their hair is still wet, for they have just finished swimming practice. The girl on the front seat beside me is reading the directions aloud as I drive down a deserted highway, past darkened stores and the occasional remaining farm.

"Up ahead a mile or so," she directs, peering at the directions with a small flashlight. "Turn right ahead, at the Needles."

"No!" Behind me I hear a girl's whispered cry. My eyes meet hers in my rearview mirror. Hers are bright with fear. Dark, wet curls frame her pretty face. "No," she repeats. "I hate going near a Needles, all dark and deserted."

The other girls fall silent, waiting to hear. "Once at a Needles near where I used to live, a little girl was killed one night by a crazy person who held her head in a puddle of water."

The blond girl who has been reading the directions shudders and looks away, out into the darkness.

In a whisper cracking with fear, as if unable to stop, the dark-haired girl continues.

". . . Ever since I heard it, it keeps happening . . . the nightmare . . . a moonless night. A woman drives along an ugly old highway, a woman obviously in a hurry. She's peering nervously over the steering wheel at the road beyond her headlights. She's hurrying on and on. Abruptly she stops the car and leans across the seat to open the door on the passenger side. There, in the darkness by the side of the road, a small girl stands trembling. Her wet hair clings in dark curls against her pretty face.

"Please," she says to the woman, "please take me home. I live at thirty-three Quiet Meadow Road."

"Get in. Get in. I'll deliver you." The woman sounds annoyed, as if the child has been bad.

The girl gets into the car, into the seat beside the driver, and closes the car door.

"The Needles is just up the road . . ." the woman says.

"No," pleads the girl. "Please, no. Just this one time, please take me home."

"No. No. No! Now don't whine, little girl," the woman scolds. "The Needles is just up the road."

"No. I'm afraid of the Needles." The little girl sobs, shrinking back into the seat. "A girl was murdered in back of a Needles once, by a crazy person who held her head down in a puddle of water." The little girl shakes her head, as if she can shake away the fear. "I can't go near a Needles."

"Don't be ridiculous!" snaps the woman. "And don't slump! Sit up straight in your seat. And stop putting your fingers in your mouth. It's not ladylike."

The woman looks at the girl, and her voice softens. "You know we musn't be late."

Into a dark parking lot the car bumps and rattles, then lurches to a stop, its headlights flickering yellow on greasy black puddles.

"Go on now," the woman orders.

The little girl sobs, resists.

"Don't be selfish!" the woman scolds. "Think about me. I have to drive and drive, night after night, and hear you whine!"

The woman leans across the little girl to open the car door. She pushes the child out of the car, then watches while the little girl slowly moves away from the car and walks with great hesitation across the cracked and broken asphalt of the deserted parking lot. Head down, as if she knows the way, she goes toward the overflowing garbage cans behind the Needles store.

"Go now," the woman coos. "You musn't keep your murderer waiting."

Then the woman closes the car door and drives without a backward glance out of the parking lot and onto the deserted highway. She drives fast, a woman in a hurry . . .

In the silence that follows, I realize that I have slowed the car to a crawl. I accelerate, try to breathe normally again.

Another girl in the back seat, the one wearing glasses, groans, "Ohh, Lisa. I hope that dream isn't catching."

No one laughs. I turn on my car radio to chase away the fear that fills the car. We have reached the corner.

I turn down the road to the party, turn at the corner, and drive past the red Needles sign, lit, unblinking, high above the cracked and broken asphalt of an empty parking lot.

We are safely past the store, and soon turn one corner and another, and arrive at a friendly group of houses, with doors and windows open, lanterns on the grass. Many young people stand on the lawn in little groups, talking, taking food from trays being passed by others. There is music. One group shoots basketballs into a hoop on a sturdy pole near the garage. I stop my taxi; the girls pay the fare, bid me goodnight, and turn to greet their friends.

In the light and life around their friends, the girls seem to recover their good spirits. But I, I decide to take a different road home, not the road past that Needles at the deserted corner, and so I do. I drive out into the quiet countryside.

I have not gone very far when I see ahead of me a woman in a sleek, grey car. She drives rapidly, then slowly. I am now directly behind her. She is peering nervously over her steering wheel at the roadside beyond the light from her car's headlamps. Though I am not in a hurry, her manner makes me uncomfortable, so I signal my intention to pass her. I do so, just as she slows to a stop. Glancing into my rearview mirror, I start. Was there someone, a dark-haired child cowering by the side of the road?

Surely not. I must be tired. Time to go home.